DREGS II

THE
AFTERTASTE

Rachel Jones

Rainy Arvo Press

DREGS II

About this book

Dregs II: The Aftertaste is a book that contains humour and horror in equal measure.

It explores topics that are both thought provoking and challenging.

The author may or may not have lived experience of these themes.

Caveat Lector

Contents

Perspective

Bad
Not
Good
Be
A horrible person
Don't be
Listening to others
Remember to be
Shunning everyone
Don't be
Kind to others
And a good thing is to be
Mean
Don't be
Nice
Be
Bad
Not
Good
(Now read from the bottom to the top) - *by Isaac Burgess, 11*

To Steve.
Put the kettle on.

Another Dog Poem

Weekend dogs are different dogs,
Whilst bacon odds are high.
Man's feet are slippered, soft, and still,
With their little people nigh.

Weekend dogs are wriggly dogs,
A cadence to their bark.
Suspension of the dreary week,
They bound, joyful, round the park.

Weekend dogs are helpful dogs,
Always keen to lend a paw.
They *schloop* the windows, sniff the drains,
Lick cold gravy off the floor.

Weekend dogs are snoozy dogs,
Heads resting 'neath the chair.
A Sunday feast, full belly growls,
And gas abroad the air!

Nothing You
Can Name

The rising sun brushed the hedge-tops, appearing sleepily in the eastern pink as a distant dog grumbled his breakfast demands into the burgeoning light. Tiny birds, ever hopeful of the early worm, chattered amongst themselves, adding their chorus to the morning refrain.

Night retreated silently into itself, gathering secrets and promises whispered under its sombre watch. In its wake, day stepped in, growing louder and brighter with each passing moment. Colour returned to the world; the full spectrum restored once more.

Through his bedroom window, Sidney Strudwick beheld the dawn's creeping progress. On the opposite wall, the light rose higher and higher, illuminating the wallpaper roses. Beryl said it was like the new day painted the bedroom, announcing "Curtain Up" on a new show. She always loved the eastern aspect of this room.

Sid could only ever catch Beryl's "show" on Sundays. Most days, he was up and out while it was still dark. Nobody wanted their milk delivered at lunchtime, especially if they

3

needed it for breakfast. He usually left the depot by dawn; milk float clinking and rattling behind him.

That was then, though. Now, in retirement, he watched the dawn's overture every day, alone.

Next door, in the potting shed, George bashed his knee on the bench. The little workspace was too small, and he found himself constantly knocking elbows and knees on something. It didn't help that finding anything in the increasing chaos was becoming a treasure hunt. Sadly, the prizes were terrible.

He ran his hand along the rough sides of the wooden bench until he found the smooth, cold metal curves of the lawnmower's handle. With a few tugs, he manoeuvred it out through the narrow doorway, pulling it free of the rest of the jumble. Squinting into the fuel tank, he noted there was plenty of petrol left to accomplish his planned chores. Out of habit, he grabbed his safety gear from the hook.

He had set himself an early start today, keen to finish everything by lunchtime. There was a county cricket match this afternoon, and he might as well get some enjoyment out of his bloody TV licence fee; the so-called entertainment tax they forced him to pay.

Death and taxes. You can't avoid either of them, he mused.

With the shed door slammed behind him, he wheeled the mower to the lawn. Looking to the kitchen window, he half expected to see Ann at the sink, washing dishes, waving and smiling. The space remained empty, of course. He missed her;

these last eight months agonising. He would give anything to see her face at the steamy window once more.

Sometimes, though, he felt her presence when struggling with the crossword. He imagined her laughing as he failed to get more than halfway through the cryptic clues. She was always the thinker, the creative flame. George was the rock on which she stood, she called him her steadfast, her clifftop.

How he longed to have Ann scold him for doing too much, to fuss over his holey socks, or even remind him to be kinder to Hissing Sid next door.

Bloody Sid, why be kind to him? They had lived through over twenty-five years of that tootling bastard leaving the house in the middle of the night. Whistling tunelessly, and always the same song, "Nothing like a Dame". Rogers and Hammerstein would be spinning in their graves to hear it. South Pacific? More like South London.

George really thought of him as *Pissing* Sid, having seen him piddle into Ann's lavender bush late one summer evening. His only consolation was that Sid obviously had problems urinating at will, his reduced stream barely dribbling into the plant pot.

Saying a silent prayer to the patron saint of prostate problems, George had allowed himself a quiet smile as he pictured Sid's urological journey over the coming years.

"Keep your friends close and your enemies closer," George said quietly, pushing the mower to a suitable starting point. Opening the choke, he pulled the starter cord. The two-stroke engine sputtered once, twice, then died.

Damn this thing.

He pulled the cord again. The same sputtering, some rumbling, then silence. It had only been a month, or perhaps six weeks since he last used it. Maybe two months? He could not remember and did not care to figure it out.

"Just bloody work, will you?" he said, clenching his jaw in angry frustration.

He pulled again. With a sputter and not a little complaining, the tiny engine finally caught, letting out a low growl before settling into a regular beat.

"At last!" said George, flipping his ear protectors into place.

Beginning his first, precise line in the lawn, he patiently walked towards the back fence from the house. There was something comforting about the forward motion, the sharp green smell soothing.

Maybe I should just mow my cares away?

The sudden roar of a lawnmower caused Sid to jump, spilling some of his tea in shock. He checked the time; just shy of six o'clock. He knew exactly who would mow their lawn at this early hour—Dr. "Pompous" Paxton next door. Paxton never missed an opportunity to show off his newest purchase or latest gadget. He was so desperate for attention, it infuriated Sid.

When they first moved into the street, the Paxtons made a point of welcoming Sid and Beryl to the neighbourhood. Then, the patronising began. Dr Paxton (*please* call me George) revelled in showing off his vinyl-upholstered cocktail cabinet and new wall-to-wall carpeting. And that was just the beginning. It seemed there was always something he wanted to boast about.

But it didn't stop there. The educated Doctor enjoyed making fun of the milkman Sid. Like how he pointed out that one man smelt of cologne, the other of sour milk and sweat. It had been fine for the wives; Beryl got on well with Ann. It was just George and Sid who hated each other at first sight.

While both men were still of working age, it was easy to avoid each other. Sundays, however, were a different matter. With roast dinners being prepared inside respective houses; in the garden, a war of attrition waged.

Sid recalled the many times he suspected George of sneaking through the dividing hedge to damage his vegetables. One summer, the other man had cut all the twine on his runner bean frames. The whole lot collapsed, and Sid salvaged nothing after the birds and snails had already feasted for a full day. George was also likely responsible for the pigeon in the water-butt (1982) and the failure of his strawberries in 1993, along with many other acts of devastation throughout the year. Every time, George was more brazen and destructive than before.

Even as Beryl lay in her last few months, watching the sunrises from her deathbed, George's campaign of destruction continued. Sid swore he would take his revenge on the awful man, the one who robbed Beryl of her final peace by firing up new-fangled purchases regularly at dawn. Chasing the birds away mid chorus and carelessly wafting noxious chemicals into her open window. For this, he would make him suffer and suffer forever.

Now, the selfish idiot was mowing his lawn at six o'clock in the morning. George hadn't gardened for a while. Sid recalled he'd been in hospital for something, and he secretly hoped it was painful. But here he came again, an inconsiderate old bastard, up to his usual tricks.

Sid headed for the back door, shaking with anger. Apoplectic and ready to burst, every muscle in his body tense, adrenaline rushing through him.

Showtime!

George spun the mower around, tracking back towards the house. Concentrating on mowing in parallel with the first line, he did not notice Sid push through the hedge separating the two properties.

Eventually though, he spotted his foe stomping across the lawn. He was red in the face and shouting something George could not make out. With over three decades' worth of insults to draw on, George could only imagine what Sid screamed at him.

This intolerable man had been a blight on George's life for a long time now. It was almost a relief to have been so deep in his grief over Ann. It meant he had stopped caring about his poisonous neighbour for a while.

The man was clearly insane and had been the entire time he had lived next door. He made Ann cry many times with his ranting and raving, and George would never forgive him for that, for spoiling her happy world. Ann tried to play it down, saying that he reminded her of her father, and it wasn't Sid's fault. But George knew better. Sid was the one that peed in the lavender pots and threw the gnomes into the pond. He also suspected it was Sid that unlocked the front gate so that Ann's little dog, Truffles, ran away, never to return. George would never forget.

George hated him.

As Sid approached, George turned the mower off and removed his ear coverings.

"Do you know what time it is, you bastard?" Sid raged.

"A little after six," George replied.

"It's too early to be running a mower!"

"Says who?"

"There's a law about it!"

"Is there, Sid?" George walked towards his back door, ignoring the angry man.

"Hey! I'm talking to you! Where are you going?"

"I need a drink of water."

"You think you're so much better than me, don't you?" spat Sid, sweat beading his brow. "Stuck up bastard!"

"Go away, you ridiculous little man. I can't deal with you today."

"Stop the noise. Stop. The noise—too early for—" Sid seemed to run out of steam. "Noise—early—"

"I'll do what I like," said George, opening the door.

From behind him came a loud thump. George flinched, unsure of his neighbour's actions. He looked round to find Sid splayed out on the ground, ashen, tearing at the collar of his shirt. He was gasping like a fish landed on a boat deck.

"Ha! Sod you, Sid!" called George. "About time you got some of your own medicine!"

He imagined Ann beside him, her face contorted with worry. "Be kind," she would have said. "Be kind, George!"

From within the kitchen George could have sworn he heard the sound of dishes in the sink.

In a daze, he yanked open the nearest cupboard, a large red package tumbling onto the countertop in the process.

"Sid, can you hear me?" he shouted.

The silence was broken only by the morning chorus.

George moved quickly. He grabbed the pack and ripped it apart, exposing the defibrillator and its attachments. Rushing over, he tore the other man's shirt open to the waist and applied two sticky pads to his chest. He turned the machine on, and it squawked to life, the electronic voice providing directions.

Whilst the device cycled through its routine, George grabbed his phone, switched it to speaker, and called an ambulance. He searched for Sid's pulse, failing to find it and unable to detect any breathing. Beginning CPR, he knew the chances of revival were slim.

Thirty compressions to two rescue breaths, cycle after cycle. Finally ready, the machine checked for shockable rhythms and did its thing. George continued CPR, ribs cracking beneath his hands, turning Sid's chest concave, saliva bubbling at his lips.

George's arms were becoming tired, so tired. He was not a young man anymore. Still, he persevered, unwilling to give up without a fight. As instructed by the machine, he stood clear again whilst it administered a shock. He felt for a pulse once more.

YES, YES! Sid had a pulse. Faint and thready, but present. He checked and grinned at the rise and fall of Sid's chest as he began taking shallow breaths. Rolling Sid on his side, George tilted his head up to keep his airway open.

"Wha—?" Sid mumbled coming back to consciousness.

"The ambulance is coming, Sid. You'll be OK."

"But you, you—"

"Yes, you utter bastard. I saved you."

"W-Why?" gasped Sid.

"I don't know, probably because I'm an old fool."

"George?" Sid whispered hoarsely.

"Yes, Sid," George said, leaning closer. He struggled to hear the man over the sound of approaching sirens.

"N-n-not thank you— just kiss my arse."

"I expected nothing less from you," replied George. "Now, thanks to *you*, I've got *two* back lawns to mow before the cricket starts."

Proof of Death

Myrtle's breath hung in the frigid air. Her unanswered question resolved by its visibility. It was, officially, flipping cold.

"Great!" she said, the sarcastic outburst lingering for a second, suspended cloud-like, before dispersing in the icy room.

For a few seconds, wrapped in her eiderdown, she considered calling in sick, blaming the weather and her arthritic knees for her absence. She would apologise profusely before spending the day tucked in her bed, listening to an audio book, guilt-free.

Then she remembered that idiot Leo. He of the wavy hair, intense gaze, and smouldering testosterone. Long past any sparks reigniting her embers, Myrtle simply found him irritating beyond all measure. She also knew his kind, many having come and gone during her lengthy career. They were flash-in-the-pans; too eager, invariably slapdash, and gone after a few months. They didn't always enjoy the most dignified of exits, but that was the world they lived in.

She sighed and risked one foot outside the covers; frost nipping at her toes as she hastily donned her slippers.

Reaching for her dressing gown, she swaddled herself inside the soft velour. It was a stereotypical "old lady" outfit, but this morning was too cold to prance about in a see-thru nightie. Besides, she was no nimble nymph these days, more of a rheumatic hag. Growing older was horrible. Why was no one warned of the rapid slide towards decrepitude?

She padded towards the kitchen. Tea would help with the cold, though not so much with the unending march towards death and decay.

"Oh, cheer up, you old bag!" she said to her reflection in the hallway mirror. "You're not dead yet."

It turned out to be a two-cup breakfast, accompanied by toast and Myrtle's own rhubarb jam. The contrast of tart jam and salted butter helped her mind switch to professional mode, the sensations distracting her brain from the cold.

Next was her work outfit, along with an extra pair of woollen tights under the pants. No such need for her top half; her work vest and fleecy jacket made sure of that. Also, she had the beanie to keep her ears toasty. Since it flattened out her hair, she went easy on the hairspray, wishing to avoid appearing like a wet spaniel later.

Checking she had everything she needed, she paused. After a moment of consideration, a tin of butterscotch sweets and a couple of fresh handkerchiefs went into the bottom of her bag. Just in case.

Her car keys, their Platinum Jubilee keyring reflecting the morning light peeping through the kitchen windows, hung on their usual hook. Placing them in her jacket pocket, she checked she had turned the kitchen appliances off, and headed for the front door.

"Right, let's hope this bloody car starts," she said, locking up behind her.

He had screwed up. Really screwed up. Edmond Gayle had landed in such a huge pile of shit that he could not see daylight.

You idiot. Stupid bloody idiot. Couldn't keep your trap shut, could you? His fists thumped against his head with each negative thought. *Now you're going to die. What a prick!*

He didn't want to cry, but he realised he was going to anyway. Barriers breaking, he fractured into sobs, tears, snot, and regrets.

What a waste!

More sobbing, some light squealing, and concerted snuffling.

Idiot!

Fuck!

He fought to regain his breath, the recent sounds of misery bouncing around his—*What was it? Cell?*

He wasn't sure what would happen next, not having given much thought to next steps. In all his calculations, this version of events did not happen. He had planned to receive congratulations, pats on the shoulder, maybe even a party and cake. This, *this*, was not part of any of his scenarios. *Ever.*

Now he would be for the long walk, and no one would mention him ever again. Which would be shitty since he had made friends here. *Obviously not, idiot.*

Something scratched on the other side of his door, a key clumsily placed in the lock. The mechanism creaked in protest. *I'll put some WD-40 on that later*, Edmond thought.

Then, he laughed. *No, I won't.*

The tears returned, quieter this time. He was regaining some control.

The door swung open, and a moon-faced man appeared, vainly trying to smile. His expression resembled a cappuccino, foam evilly slashed by a cinnamon grin. While attempting to seem friendly, he had transformed into a slightly menacing potato, giving Edmond the shivers.

"Alright, Ed, mate?" said the potato.

"Erm—maybe. Don't know, Brett."

"Ha, ha. That's the way. Coming for a drive then?"

"Rather not, if you don't mind?"

"No, you are coming for a drive. Alright?"

"Righto," said Edmond, standing on wobbly legs. "I might need a hand, Brett, you know—"

"Of course, mate. No problem. Bit o' stage fright, eh?"

Edmond gave a wan smile, hopping from foot to foot. "Could I just, erm, pee?"

"Yup, on the way out, me old mucker. All sorted."

"Thanks."

Potato Brett stepped forward and put a hand under Edmond's left elbow. His touch was surprisingly gentle. "I gotcha, let's go."

Edmond did not glance back as they stepped into the hallway, but he did add the squeaky lock to his To Do List.

Brett allowed him to take his final piss in private; well, *sort of* in private. His bladder was grateful, but now his stomach grumbled. He was hungry, ridiculously hungry. When was the last time he ate? What time was it now?

He only remembered being dragged out of bed and bundled away; bagged and tagged. They tossed him in what he guessed to be a van, cavernous by the sound, the diesel engine rumbling during the long drive to his place of captivity

Now, here he was, head back beneath the hood, but not in a van. It sounded much smaller, and he was strapped in by a seat belt. He wasn't too comfortable, as they had fastened his hands behind him, and he kept wriggling to stop them going to sleep. He guessed he was in a car.

The driver did not speak, only identifiable by the occasional grunt as they changed gears. They had tuned the radio to a news channel, something mainstream, possibly Radio 4.

From the traffic sounds, he thought they may have been in a country lane. He knew it was dark out, some light filtering through his hood from approaching cars, and though the journey seemed endless, it had probably only been twenty minutes or so.

Abruptly, Edmond got at least one of his wishes. The radio presenter identified herself as Leonie Pitcher of Radio 4, and it was just after two; time for a feature on preserving fruit and vegetables titled "One Jar Too Far". Ms. Pitcher—*what an apt name*, thought Edmond—began by extolling the virtues of preserving one's homegrown produce. The driver turned the volume up a little, and Edmond was grateful, able to hear more clearly now.

The presenter continued describing different fruits and whether they were economical to cultivate, given the limited space of modern housing and tiny gardens. Ms. Pitcher was all for bramble jelly, plum jam, strawberry anything, and mango chutney. However, she believed that rhubarb was not something the public wanted anymore, and suggested planting quince instead.

"Rubbish!" shouted Edmond.

"Nonsense!" came a growl from the driver's seat.

"Dig up my rhubarb, for horrible old quince? Never!"

"Stupid woman!"

"Next thing, she'll tell us to grow quinoa on the windowsill."

"Or avocados in the conservatory!"

"They should leave our jams alone. Modern nonsense. Honestly!" said Edmond.

"You're not wrong," the driver said.

Edmond cocked his head to one side. "Sorry to be so intrusive, especially in this day and age—but are you a lady driver?"

There was a sharp intake of breath, followed by a short silence.

Finally, they spoke. "Yes, yes, I am. I'm so sorry. I shouldn't have said anything. It's against my code."

"Your code? Like a code of silence?"

"No, not really. Code of Conduct. For contract kills and so on."

"Oh."

"You are only the second person I have ever spoken to, if I'm honest. It is easier that way, you know?"

"Oh, I expect it is," said Edmond, wriggling a little to encourage the circulation in his hands. "Funny kind of job though, isn't it?"

"It is, nowadays. All gang and drug money stuff. Not like before."

"I agree. In the old days, it was diamonds, bearer bonds, and corrupt police."

"I do miss our bent Bobbies. Streets were much safer then, I think."

"Absolutely. Now we have drug trafficking, human trafficking, organ trafficking, and global crime syndicates. It has all gone to hell."

"Not to mention having to knock off people wanting to get out, unwilling to play the game anymore. They should just let them go."

"That's why I'm sitting here. I told them, I am too old for this. I don't want to look after stolen kidneys or babysit Moldavian labourers. I didn't mind a little bag of twinkly stones or a suitcase full of cash, but people are not things to be bought and sold. It isn't for me. But apparently, I have seen too much and now need to take the long walk."

He sighed inside his hood. He hadn't realised that, as well as being afraid, he was quite pissed off. In all his years, he never once spoke out of turn, and wasn't planning to either.

"I'm trying to get out, too," she said. "I have no problem taking out the nasties, even though they are some mother's son. I kept the streets free of those who preyed on the weak and vulnerable. Which was good, until I realised I was the predator, even if I tried to fool myself I was only a contractor. The last straw was a twenty-year-old girl who had escaped her manager."

"Oh no! Did you kill her?"

"Nope. I gave the job to Leo. He enjoyed it, too. Filthy business."

The car pulled over before slowing to a stop, and the driver exhaled. There was a creak as she leant backwards across her seat, then a wash of light as she lifted his hood.

Peat dark eyes, set amongst creases and crows' feet, examined him from beneath silvery hair tucked under a black woollen beanie. A smile blossomed across her lips, and Edmond had the impression it was always there, waiting, let loose, along with the laughter overtaking her, only when she wanted.

She put out her hand. "I'm Myrtle."

"Oh, er, apologies, can't—" Edmond wiggled in his seat, contorting in an attempt to shake her hand.

"Oh, I'm so sorry. Here let me—"

She took a knife from her bag, wiped it with a blue, floral hankie, and cut the ties on his wrists. The relief was immediate, and he brought his hands forwards to rub them, trying to get the circulation going again.

"Myrtle, I'm Edmond," he said. "Sorry I didn't meet you before. We could have been firm friends."

She shook a tin at him. "Butterscotch? Afraid it's just about all I've got."

He reached into the mound of sweets, taking one and then

a second when she gestured for him to do so. In his mouth, the sugary caramel drifted silk-like over his tongue, tasting like love. It appeared he would die happy.

Butterscotch happy.

"Thank you," he said, "that is truly kind. Would it be alright if we got this over and done with? I'm feeling relaxed, but I might need to pee again in a minute."

"I've got a bladder like that," she said.

Myrtle chuckled and rummaged in her bag before pulling out a small jar labelled "Strawberry". Popping the lid with the knife, she caught some on the blade and offered it to Edmond.

"Last summer's," she said.

He took the knife and carefully pressed the flat edge to his upper lips, scraping off a little of the sticky substance. The taste leapt into his mouth, doing obscene things to his senses, and having an unrestrained jam orgy on his tongue.
His eyes rolled back into his head and he almost swooned.

"Good, isn't it?" said Myrtle.

"Amazing!" said a breathless Edmond, handing over the blade.

"Right, now we've got our jams in order, here's the plan—"

Leo could not be more pleased, smarming around the office like a post-coital jackal. Finally, the old bat had 'retired', and he was rightfully on top. Where he belonged, of course.

In the end, it was a massive stroke after that last job that did for poor Myrtle, and doctors said there was no chance of recovery, ever. Leo still laughed on the inside, despite the flowers and sympathy cards scattered around the office. Silly old bitch. She should have pegged it years ago.

He packed away the files from that final job; *Edward somebody-blah.* The proof of death picture showed him spread-eagled in the undergrowth, red flowers blooming across a yellow shirt, his head wedged between some tree roots. Silly cow must have tried to drag him out. No wonder she blew a gasket.

At least she had sent the picture before ditching the phone, although her last text was too garbled to read. The boys had traced it to some little country hospital, where an elderly woman matching her description was "very poorly after a massive stroke".

Poor Jane Doe.

Leo smiled again. How *dreadfully* sad.

The dark red flowers stained the fabric, stubbornly refusing erasure.

"I'm never getting the jam out of this," she said, giggling, holding the yellow shirt up for him to see before hanging it on the line.

He looked up, enjoying the way her hair rippled, ocean-like, in the breeze. They shared a smile, basking in the lives they had reclaimed.

Returning his attention to the garden, he found the vibrant purple stalks and bold green umbrellas of the rhubarb patch positively daring him to turn them into jam. He laughed, stripping the leaves from the plants.

"Rhubarb, not *quince?* Heaven preserve us!" he said into the warm, Hebridean air.

And preserve them he did, making sure to label the jars, "Rhubarb – Year One".

Screaming In The Shower

Because no one sees.
Because no one hears.
Because I don't know
whether to shave my legs
or sever my throat.
Because no one saw.
Because no one heard
Because rending my wet skin
does not ease the ache
of deep shame.
Because a shower won't drown me.
Believe me, I tried.
It only baptises my pain,
absolving it to sin again.
You are never forgiven.
And,
because of you.
I still scream.

Fishing in the Dark

"I hate these boots!" Grant complained, flinging them against the wall.

"Bloody boots, bloody hat, bloody fishing rod!" He announced each item as they followed the first across the room with resounding thuds.

"I'm not going! What's the point?!"

His mum peeped around the door, and seeing her son's tantrum, quickly withdrew. "Graham," she called, "Come and have a word, will you?"

Appearing in the hallway, her husband said, "Alright, love, I'll handle it," before stepping into the maelstrom.

At first, he didn't see Grant. Then, drawn by muffled shouting, he spotted a pair of feet protruding from the blankets. Grabbing one of them, he mercilessly tickled it. Grant swore, loudly.

"I'll have none of that language, boy," said his dad, pulling hard on each toe.

"Aargh! Let me go, Dad, please!"

"Only if you stop behaving like a milksop."

Grant sat up with as much enthusiasm as a sack of grumpy

spuds. He ground his young teeth in frustration, the metallic sound clanging around the quiet room.

"Do I have to do it? What's the point?"

"Son, we're gnomes. We are a noble race. Our kings once ruled the world and our future—"

"—was bright. Yeah, I know. I get that, and I love it. But that—" he gestured to the discarded outfit, "—is so cheesy."

"It's the way things are. We've all done it."

"I thought my first campaign would be more, well, more heroic an' all."

"Oh, you'll get your mettle tested, that's for sure."

"But I want to be a Battle Gnome; it's all I've ever—"

"I know. For now, you're doing this. Get dressed. I'll drop you off at the Garrison."

Grant stood, shoulders slumped. "Yes, Dad."

Ginny was waiting at the door as Graham came out. "Is he alright?" she asked.

"It's just his age," said Graham. "I went through the same when I turned three hundred."

Ginny appeared unconvinced.

Graham lifted her chin. "I promise, my love. He'll be right as raindrops in no time."

Smiling, she nodded to a lunch bag squealing and wriggling on the kitchen counter. "I've made him something special to eat."

"Oh, he does love his rodents, 'specially the lively ones. That'll cheer him up," he said, reaching for the back door. "I'll hitch the weasel up. Don't want the boy late on his first night."

"I feel stupid." Grant's mood had not improved.

"You look splendid, son. I couldn't be prouder."

They sat in silence for a while, the dusk cool as they travelled through it. Valentine, the weasel, bounded along, pulling the buggy haphazardly over bumps and ruts, apologising profusely.

"Look at me, dressed like this," moaned Grant.

"It's what you're born'd to do, son. Like I was, and all our kind,"

Grant plucked at his shirt and pouted loudly. He hated this.

"We're getting close, boss," said Valentine as he slowed to a trot, the Garrison coming into view a moment later, its turrets glowering before the setting sun. Arriving at the front gates, Grant hopped down from the buggy, trying to smile.

"Got everything, son?"

Grant patted his enormous, squirming lunch bag. "Yup, guess so."

"See you in the morning," Graham said. "Cheer up, will you? I'd love to be your age again!" Then, whistling to the weasel, who winked encouragingly at Grant, he pulled away from the kerb.

A large group of gnomes stood around the muster room, chatting excitedly. Grant, however, picked a spot in the shadows. He hated looking like this; it was humiliating.

Concealing himself behind his lunch bag, he considered the contents. What feast had his mother packed for him? He hoped it was shrews. Crunching those little beasties would be something to look forward to this evening.

He was deeply proud of his Gnomeage, and had whole-heartedly committed to his teeth filing ceremony. For goodness' sake, he had even spent a year delivering daffodils to the Bridge Trolls as part of an ancient something or other. But, being done up in this new outfit was beyond his comfort zone.

Black. What kind of self-respecting gnome wore black?

He pined for his blue trousers, yellow jerkin, and red hat.

His dad had once told him that black was the absence of light, not a real colour. Now, here he was, in black boots, pants, and shirt.

What a loser.

He glanced at the other occupants of the room. Everyone was in black. It was depressing.

With any luck, I'll catch Gneumonia and die before the end of the week, he thought.

Someone jabbed him in the ribs, and Grant spun round to face a young girl with a cheeky grin and eyes the colour of pondweed.

"Cheer up, mizzog! Tonight's going to be fun!"

"Really? I don't think so," said Grant. "It's pretty bleak, so far."

"It's what you make it. Sixth time round for me. I love it."

"Well, good for you." He turned away.

Another jab in the ribs, harder this time.

"Oi! Stop that!" he snapped.

"Shan't. Not 'til you smile. Next poke will make you burp, so don't make me do it."

"Can't you go annoy another gnome? I'm trying to, well, trying to—"

"What, sulk like a ninny? You're doing well." She poked him in the belly again. He burped.

"That's it," she said. "Feel better now? Big bag o'wind."

She held out a hand to Grant. "The name's Laxxi. Short for Galaxy, and long for Lax."

He shook it without enthusiasm. "I'm Grant. The long and short of it."

The pondweed swirled momentarily, her gaze fixed on him. "You'll do," she said.

A loud *TAP-TAP-TAP* silenced the room as an imposing Elder Gnome called everyone to order. He too was dressed from hat to boots in black, but not in the cheap outfits the others wore. Black velvet, held together by midnight stitching and obsidian buttons draped over him, and Grant angled for a better view.

"That's Gideon. He's in charge," whispered Laxxi. "He's four thousand years old."

Gideon cleared his throat and began speaking, the words an ancient tongue Grant couldn't understand.

Quickly, a rooster hopped to the old Gnome's side and *bok-bokked* in his ear.

Gideon restarted. "I do apologise. I find myself lost in language these days. Let us begin again." He coughed quietly.

"I am Gideon," he said. "Commander of this Garrison. Welcome to you all, especially our new members. I founded the very first Gnight Patrol many summers ago. It saved us then, and it continues to do so now."

Something in the old Gnome's voice reminded Grant of leaves underfoot. There was a familiarity there he could not quite recognise, but it left him feeling gently swaddled.

The Commander continued, "It is incumbent upon every young gnome to enter our forces once they turn three hundred; a Gnational Service if you will. Your community will be ever thankful for your contribution as you keep us all safe."

The crowd murmured, nudging each other.

"Not all of you are thrilled to be here. It is hard to leave the colourful homes and hearths you love, and difficult to stand, clothed in darkness. Remember, we only come out at night, dear ones." He paused, examining the attentive faces. "You will understand why all this bleakness is necessary once you step into the dusky world above our homelands."

"It's brilliant out there," Laxxi muttered to Grant.

"So, be brave and bold. Strike first and strike hard. Sgt. Biped oversees the operation and has my full authority and trust. Good luck to you all."

He doffed his hat towards the feathered Sergeant before taking his leave.

"Right," crowed Biped, "let's allocate the badgers and head out."

For logistical purposes, Grant and Laxxi had been paired up. Or rather, Laxxi was asked to babysit Grant on his first patrol. They were given Gruncheon, an indifferent badger, and were soon en route to the site of their first job: an address "Up Top" in Market Hale, Essex.

Promptly crossing to the over-world via the West Essex portal, they pottered along the dark pavements of the small town in silence.

"What if we're seen?" whispered Grant.

Laxxi giggled, and leant forwards to Gruncheon's ear. "D'ya hear that, Grunch? He thinks we'll be spotted!"

The badger snorted in derision. "As if!" he rumbled.

Laxxi spoke over her shoulder, "Silly billy! Why do you think we are darker than a soot-storm? Why are we taking a badger when weasels are quicker?" She faced the front again. "No offence, Grunch."

"None taken, I s'pose."

"We can't be seen when we are without colour, Grant. It's the law or something."

"Oh," said Grant. He caught a whiff of something unpleasant, probably humans, and shuddered at the thought.

"We slip in during the night. Do our thing and leave. It's a bit of a lark, really!"

"Right."

Gruncheon plodded on, the regular rhythm of the badger's gait calming. Maybe this night would be alright after all. He was becoming more accustomed to the gloom surrounding them and could easily close his eyes for a minute or two. If it weren't for the stench.

"We're here!" said the badger, letting them dismount. "Hurry up. My dinner's waiting, if it hasn't already slithered off."

The two gnomes stood by the kerb.

"We'll be as quick as we can," said Laxxi. "Listen for my call."

Pulling a piece of parchment from her pocket, she studied it before checking her watch and peering at the row of bungalows across the street. "We need number eleven." Spotting the correct property, she scampered over, Grant on her heels.

The garden gate was ajar, and she squeezed through the gap, beckoning Grant on. He followed, tripping over his boots to fall through the opening.

"Sssh! Noisy boy!" said Laxxi, finger to her lips. "Keep behind me."

They nipped, ducked and scurried up the front path, arriving at the doorstep quickly. It was really, properly dark now, and Grant didn't much like it. Night was for sleeping, not all this creeping about. Gnomes shouldn't be out at night.

He remembered the tales of gnomes toasted to death by the light of the silvery moon, and adding the gnomes eaten by cats, drowned in ponds, and maimed by sparrows just confirmed it was a dangerous world up here. A fight for survival, in fact. There was even talk of humans, vicious beasts that they were, smiting gnomes for fun.

It was horrific, this world plagued by other creatures, the most merciless of which was humankind.

"Hello?" called Laxxi into the shadows. "You there?"

Silence.

"We're the Gnight Patrol," she said.

"Show yourself and name your clan," a voice said from the darkness.

Laxxi stepped forward. "I'm Galaxy, daughter of Giovanni and Grunhilde Acorn. We claim blood with Pond-Leaf."

"What about him?"

Laxxi waved Grant forward. "Tell them."

"I'm Grant, son of Graham and Ginny Wheatear. We claim blood with First Snow."

A ruddy-cheeked gnome stepped from the shadows, open-handed. "Welcome," he said, "I'm Geoff Flint, of Fernshadow. I'll not introduce the others."

Laxxi nodded at the brightly coloured figure, clearly visible in the half-light. "Pleased to meet you, sorry about the situation. Best step back into the shadows, though," she said. "I'm guessing they'll be here in the next few minutes?"

"Yes." Geoff sounded bereft. "Just like every Friday, when their pubs shut."

Anger whirled in Laxxi's calm eyes. "Bloody humans!" she said, her brow screwed tight in thought.

"Right," she said. "Grant, go to the pond, pick up a rod, and start fishing."

"In the dark?"

"It's part of the Laxxi Masterplan; don't panic." Her smile was evident in her voice.

Grant headed pondward.

"Geoff, that's one spot covered, where else?"

"By the lavender bush, if you can find it." He pointed into the gloom.

"I can smell where it is. Go inside, mate. We'll deal with this."

Geoff wasted no time in hurrying away.

"Grant, when they get here, bite anything that comes near you, OK? You have permission to use your battle-jaw."

"I thought that was only—"

"Use it widely and wisely. It's how we defend our own."

"OK, but—"

"Sssh! Here they come."

Raucous laughter drifted from the street.

"Grunch, be ready to go!" she called.

"As always," the badger called back.

Footsteps drew closer, and the gate swung open, hinges shrieking in protest. Two men entered, giggling and stumbling.

"Time for a little Gnome improvement," one said, heading for Grant.

"Bash its horrible head in," said the other, making a bee-line for Laxxi. He bent down and picked her up. "Here, this one's a funny colour—"

Grant felt himself being lifted to eye-level. "So's this one—"

"Mine's moving, it's squirming, it's—Aargh!"

"What?"

"It bit me!"

"You're drunk. How can it bite you? It's just a stupid, concrete gnome."

Grant's spine straightened, steel filling his vertebrae. In his mouth, saw-teeth ascended from his jaw, and small, razor-sharp incisors appeared beneath his curled lips.

He stared at the ugly, soulless human. This thing was the real blight on his beautiful world.

Nearby, Laxxi began to devour her foe's hand, munching

her way up his arm. The crunching of bone made Grant drool in anticipation.

"Help! It's got me—"

Grant's captor was frozen in horror, and fearing that the fool would drop him, Grant hissed loudly. "Psst! Psst! Look!"

The man turned, eye to furious eye with Grant. The young gnome's jaw opened, mandible dislocating to increase the angle of his maw. Leaping from the human's grip, he fell upon him, clamping his legs around the man's neck. Grant shut his mouth tight, snapping the beast's head off in one fell swoop, mashing and mangling his jaw down through the human's frame.

Grant realised that, in this moment of ferocity, his ancestors gathered round him, shadow forms of granite eyes, iron jaws, and blood-stained faces. The vision was terrifying, but they were staring at the carnage, seemingly pleased by it. So, he continued, biting and swallowing and chewing until there was nothing left.

The man tasted good, like rainy Tuesdays; warm and a little salty.

Delicious.

Once he had ground everything into paste, he spat out a viscous, strawberry-coloured stream of blended bone and tissue to form a little upturned cone of a person on the dark ground. *Not a bad shade of pink. I wonder if I can find a neckerchief in this colour.*

Laxxi bounded over. "Well done, Gnewbie! Excellent work!"

Grant, a little shaky, sat with a bump. He was lost in the intensity of the experience, not sure if he felt triumph or disgust.

"You'll be OK," said Laxxi. "First time's always a bit weird."

Triumph or disgust? Pride or shame? Right or wrong?

Laxxi shook his arm, bringing his world back into focus.

Triumph it was.

"Are you kidding me?" Grant grinned. "I saw the ancestors, and they were smiling!"

Laxxi squealed with joy. "That's amazing, what an honour!"

"It felt right, Lax. I felt like it was what I was meant to do."

Gruncheon poked his snout over the wall and snuffed. "It's getting early. We've got a curfew. Only allowed to come out at night, that's what the Old Gnome said."

Laxxi pulled a smiling Grant to his feet. "He's right, of course." Skipping ahead, she said, "Same again tomorrow, if you like?"

Grant caught her up. "Yeah, but can I sit up front? I'm quite sure Gruncheon farts."

"No, I don't!" huffed the badger.

"Yes, you do," they both replied, clambering up on his back.

"I can't help myself. It's the organic slugs the missus gives me."

"Whatever, Grunch, you've always farted." said Laxxi.

"Would you both prefer to walk home?"

Silence.

"I thought not!" he said as he trotted away.

PFFFT!

"Oops. S'cuse me!"

And then, they were gone.

Well, all apart from the smell.

A Gnome's Request

Once a month, our Moon shines full,
O'er town and field and marsh.
But us old-timer moanin' Gnomes,
Find her light a little harsh.

Please be so kind and stop a while,
to help adjust our dress.
We'll be very grateful for your time
and gentle thoughtfulness.

A little cape, a tiny hood
– that's all we need tonight.
Then we can slumber peacefully
whilst Sister Moon is bright.

Father's Day

It was *his* day.

Most people called a birthday their special day, not Harvey. He was unfortunate enough to share a birthday with his son. He therefore was made to relinquish all claims over the second of June, seceding to his only born child. As a consolation prize, he had been awarded Father's Day as the day he could call his own. Let the celebrations begin. Truthfully, he would prefer to be left alone with his latest book purchase and a cup of tea.

Earlier, he had awoken to the sound of his spouse hawking up her morning phlegm, retching, and coughing into the basin. The bathroom door ajar, he glimpsed the flesh mountain reverberating with each expulsion. Before the lovely Madeline could insist that he received his celebratory hump and positional asphyxia, he donned his slippers. He padded down to the safety of his kitchen, and peace.

His light step became leaden as he caught sight of his son slouched across the kitchen counter. He appeared to be sleeping, drooling on Harvey's stack of gardening brochures. Propped up on the stool, half-dressed.

"Roland!" he said. No response from the sleeper. "Roland, wake up!"

Roland made a smacking noise with his lips and fluttered his eyelids. He slept on. Harvey stepped forward, brought his mouth close to his son's ear, and whispered, "Wake up!"

Roland snapped upright, a colourful page plastered to his face. He had become a grotesque billboard advertising "All Dad's Garden Gifts- Now on Sale at Duncan's Depot!". Roland turned his bleary eyes towards his dad. He did not appear to be fully awake. He peeled the page away from his skin.

"I'm going to bed," he mumbled. "Too much noise."

From the doorway, a voice boomed, "Roland, go wash up and be ready to leave in fifteen minutes!"

Madeline stood, hands on hips, chest out in the manner of a matador--if matadors were three hundred pounds and wore housecoats.

"Today is Father's Day, and we are taking Dad out for a treat."

"Why? He won't like it. He's not interested," said Roland. "Take me out instead. He can tag along like the loser he is."

Harvey said nothing. He didn't want to be in the company of these two. They didn't want to be with him, either.

"Your Dad likes to enjoy himself once a year. This is the day."

"Well, don't let him dress like a creep, Mom. Everyone stares."

"I'll do my best with him. We can always pretend he's from out of state, I suppose." She giggled.

"I *can* hear both of you, you know," said Harvey.

"Never mind, dear," said his wife. "You shower and I'll come help you dress."

"Not like a freak, please Mom," said Roland, bounding up the stairs to beat Harvey to the bathroom.

How wonderful, thought Harvey. *No hot water left for me again.*

The drive to the shopping mall was mercifully short. The time spent waiting for Roland to flit in and out of every sports shop (Harvey had counted sixteen) seemed endless. Sadly, Roland had also run into a couple of friends from college. Harvey only realised this when he was shunted into a service doorway to stand behind Madeline's bulk, hidden from sight. Five minutes and a multitude of *Yeah, bro's* later, he was dragged back into the main thoroughfare.

He glared at the back of his son's head, keeping the obligatory five paces behind him. His wife continually fussing over her "baby" as they walked towards the exits.

I could just turn around and head the other way, thought Harvey. They wouldn't even notice.

As if to prove she could read his mind, Madeline turned around to scowl at him. Realising he was getting too close to the pair, he slowed his pace. He resumed gazing vacantly at the shop displays and smiling at the happier families walking their way. Madeline turned again.

"Stop smiling. You look like a pervert," she hissed.

Harvey bowed his head, shamed once more. He tried to

be invisible, but even the magical powers of Father's Day couldn't help with his request.

At least he would spend a happy hour in Duncan's Depot. Something to look forward to. He knew a couple of things he might pick up in the sale. This might be something positive from this awful day. He smiled, then remembered he was not supposed to do so. He hung his face on an imaginary hook and let it sag, expressionless.

Just being in the cavernous store gave Harvey a thrill. The woody air, tinged with paint, wafted all around with hints of solvent and adhesive. A heady scent, Harvey liked it.

Turning into the machinery aisle, his heart pounded. The object of his desire was still on sale. The bright red unit stood out against the galvanised shelving and darkened corners at this far end of the store.

He approached it, almost fearful to touch it, terrified of yet more rejection. Its surface smooth and cold under his fingertips.

"I'll be with you in a minute, sir!" came a voice from the top of a steel ladder.

"OK," Harvey replied. "I can wait."

"Oh, you can *wait*, can you, Dad? How kind of you to speak for us all. You're a joke, a bad one at that."

"Roland, please don't talk to me like—"

"Or what, you'll bore me to death with your engineering anecdotes?"

"Son, I only—"

"Only what? Should have been more interesting?"

Madeline looked amused. She had trained her boy well. He had the same disgusted sneer she wore when Harvey came near her. Those two were a pair, and he merely a canker. Alone in his own family.

"Hello, I'm Andy. How can I help you?" the ladder man appeared at ground level. He removed a pair of thick gloves and shook hands.

"Sorry to interrupt you, Andy. I'm Harvey."

"Not a problem, Harvey. Got some trouble with our cameras. I am trying to reset them. It hasn't turned out to be an easy fix, either."

"Well, if you have time, I'd like to enquire about the Diablo Deluxe. Is this one for sale?"

"Excellent choice. Yes, half price for today only. This is the last of our stock."

"Well, I'm halfway sold already!"

"Let's take a look then, Harv, shall we?"

The two men walked towards the machine, Andy giving a full rundown of what the Diablo would munch its way through if it were fed correctly.

Madeline called out, "I'm off to the coffee shop, Harvey. Find me when you're done."

Harvey waved in acknowledgement, engrossed in his own conversation. Then, to his dismay, he realised Roland had remained behind. He probably wanted to use this opportunity to humiliate him again.

"Would you like to fire her up?" asked the assistant.

Harvey's grin widened as he nodded. "That would be great!"

"We've got some scrap wood you can test it with, as well." He pointed to a pile of timber by the back wall. "That way you'll feel how it runs, get an idea of its power."

"Go on, Dad, feel some power for once," said Roland.

Harvey lowered his eyes, about to change his mind.

"Maybe I should just—"

"Maybe my dad should just go back to the car, Mr. Depot Man. He can't be trusted with a pencil, let alone heavy machinery."

The colour rose from Harvey's chest, spreading upwards. He feared he would be sick. He should be at home, reading and invisible.

Roland stooped to stare into his father's lowered face. He pulled his mouth into a malicious slash. He gave a pretend gasp.

"Oh, *no!*" he mocked, "I think Daddy peed his freaky pants. How embarrassing!"

Andy cleared his throat and addressed Harvey. "Sir, let me show you what this beautiful machine can do."

He pushed an amber button, causing an alarm to beep from the inner part of the Diablo.

"Right. It is now armed. To activate the rotating blades and make her chop and chew like a hungry bear, you need to push these two green ones at the same time."

He pushed the green buttons. The Diablo roared into life, shaking the objects on nearby shelves. Harvey felt as though he were next to a fighter jet which was preparing to take off.

It was as magnificent as he knew it would be. It would easily cope with all the yard work he had to do.

He had to have it.

Andy approached with a flat based trolley piled high with wood. "Try these," he said.

Picking up a thick plank, he fed it to the hungry machine. The plank was gone in a flash. The bucket filled with a thin layer of wood chippings. Its performance impressed Harvey. The Diablo was a magnificent machine. He made towards the woodpile.

Roland barged him out of the way. "Not for you, Dad. Much too dangerous," he said.

He picked up some timber and fed it to the machine. Pleased with himself, he crowed with delight. Harvey sighed.

"Anyhow, a couple of things to note, sir," Andy continued.

Harvey strained to hear him over the noise of Roland whooping and the monster's metallic jaws grinding.

Andy pointed to a lever on the side of the machine. "This opens the intake chute wider in case you need to insert a larger load. Also, as an emergency override, this red button is the Emergency Stop mechanism, which will turn off the motor instantly."

Harvey nodded. "Thanks. Appreciate the info."

"I only mention it because when our cameras went off-line today, we also blew some internal circuits. We haven't reset this stop button yet. We can't guarantee it will work instantly."

"Oh, *right*." Harvey said.

"Worrying really, as this corner of the store currently is without *any* safety surveillance whatsoever."

He looked into Harvey's eyes and raised his chin towards the shouting youngster mashing timber into wood chips.

"Yup, it's like the dark lands down here. Cut off. Dismembered from the rest of the store."

Harvey's eyes widened, dark as espresso.

"Oh, *right.*" he replied.

Frustrated, Madeline put her phone down. She couldn't make out anything playing on her newsfeed. Which idiot had set off a siren? Likely it was that useless fool of a husband of hers. He was such a misery to be around. This trip had been a complete waste of her time. Thankfully, it only happened once a year.

The siren wailed for a few more minutes, stopping suddenly. The instant silence ringing louder than the alarm had. She huffed in annoyance then continued to browse her phone. A smiling server brought her a fresh latte. Madeline did not acknowledge their presence.

Later, as she put her empty cup down on the table, she looked up to see her husband approaching. He was practically being carried by a pair of uniformed police officers. Harvey had turned the colour of porridge. His mouth hung loosely, his eyes blinking slowly, not focusing on anything. His hands were a pair of fledgling birds, shaking on the precipice of their first flight.

"What's happened? Have you had another turn? You're so embarrassing, Harvey." she said.

"Is this your husband, ma'am?"

She nodded.

The officers sat the crumpled man down. He slumped sideways in the tiny bistro chair.

"Ma'am, I'm afraid something serious has occurred," said the officer whose tag read 'Sgt Harris'.

"Ha! To *this* fool? He does it all the time. I'm sorry."

"No Ma'am. Your husband is fine, but he can't tell us his full name or any of your son's details."

"My son?" Madeline was confused. "What's going on?"

"Ma'am, it is important. What is your son's name?"

"Roland. Roland is my son. What's going on?" Her voice becoming shrill.

"Is that his full name?"

"No, it's Roland Trevor."

"Last name?"

"Slaywood. My son is Roland Trevor Slaywood."

"Ma'am, I'm afraid there is terrible news. Your son fell into some machinery and sustained fatal injuries. We are so sorry for your loss."

Madeline's primal howl hurtled around the huge store. The horrendous sound of grief devouring a heart, unmistakable and unavoidable.

Whilst Sgt Harris consoled the grieving mother, the second police officer spoke quietly to Harvey.

"I know you're in shock, sir. It is an awful thing. We've

talked to the assistant who served you and he described how your son was being reckless. Throwing things into the wood-chipper, ignoring his safety advice and all the warning signs."

Harvey nodded. A tear splashed on his trembling hands.

"It was a terrible, terrible accident. You must not blame yourself."

He placed a steady hand on Harvey's shoulder, patting him sympathetically.

Madeline had stopped screaming and turned her ire to-wards Harvey.

"*You* let this happen to our boy. *You* didn't save him. You useless bastard."

She sobbed and gutted, silver trails sliding from her nose and eyes.

"I never want to see you again!" Spittle flew from her mouth. It gave her the appearance of an angry snake.

"Get away from me! *Get him away from me!*" She turned her chair to face the opposite direction. Harvey stared at her angry shoulders.

Then, somewhere in the deepest, darkest dungeon of Harvey's heart, a tiny candle flickered. For the first time in over twenty years; he felt hope come alive in him once more.

He exhaled, feeling the smoke of swallowed pain leaving his body. Determination straightening his spine, ironing out years of cowering down.

I think I have just made parole; he thought.

It was time to go.

He gave his contact details to the officers; told them he

would come to the station in the morning, and that he would be fine. He stood, pushed his chair back under the table and left the coffee shop. He didn't even glance at Madeline. He didn't care. He was free.

As he got to the store entrance, he saw Andy talking to the departing customers. He approached him, unsure of what to say. The assistant smiled his way.

"Hello sir," he said. "Did you get what you needed at Duncan's Depot today?"

"Yes, Andy, I did," said Harvey with his chin up. "I'm much obliged to you."

They shook hands. Harvey walked into the daylight, towards the car (*his* car) trying not to smile at the people gathered in the parking lot.

He wondered where he would take himself for lunch. He remembered the coffee shop next to his favourite bookstore.

Perfect!

This was turning out to be the best Father's Day ever.

Sweeping In The Dark

Darling
I'm so sorry
To keep
From you the
Nature of
The blades
That flicked
The flames
That licked
The beasts
That hate.

Darling
I'm so sorry
To hide
Within the
Feelings that
The words
That shamed

The fear
That claimed
The light
It ate.

Darling
I'm so sorry
To say
(but) Not aloud
In the pit
The voice
That screams
The end
Of dreams
The beating down
Of fate.

My darling
I'm so sorry
That
You love
Me but
I make
You spend
Your days
Sweeping
In
The
Dark

Seen But Not Heard

The foamy water in the bowl bubbled the skin from her hands and lower arms. The heat distorted into agony as she succumbed to the first waves of excruciating pain. She remained silent. Pursing her lips, clenching her teeth, and screwing her eyes tight. She would not whimper, squeal, or cry out. She would give him nothing about which to comment.

She removed her hands from the water, the suds continuing to scorch as she dripped onto the dishes below. Her smoked salmon limbs, scalded from just below the elbow, shone and burnt. She held her screams inside. She was not willing to hear his mocking tone, his little four-word ditty.

Holding the tea towels under the cold tap for a few seconds, she knew she would feel relief before long. She leant on the draining board and wrapped the cool cloths around her seared arms. This was a tender swaddling process as her every nerve ending jangled at the merest brush against her shocked tissue.

She exhaled, controlling her breath. A muted hiss puffed through her half-open lips. Her stinging extremities cooled, still delivering harsh, burning pain every few moments. The time for screaming had passed, though, for that she was grateful.

Turning from the sink, she checked the contents of the tray. Sandwich, coffee, biscuits, and an apricot—everything was in place. She gently unwound the tea towels and rolled down her sleeves, lifting the tray to her hip on her way past.

Padding along the hallway, her slippers made soft scuffs on the carpet beneath her feet. Not really the sound of footsteps, more like the sound of clouds bumping into marshmallows. She smiled. Maybe she lived in a children's show where all the noises were funny, and nothing ever went *Bang!* There would certainly be no screaming or the sound of a hammer on flesh.

She stopped smiling.

As she stepped into the lounge, she saw him in his full glory. He half-sat, half-slouched in his recliner; his cotton shirt had ridden up, exposing the fleshy belly of someone who was fond of the high life. His tight waistband pinched him in half, proving that his epicurean lifestyle also demanded considerable investment in keeping fit. The only shortcut to Hedonism was through the dangerous Valley of the Glutton. It looked like he had ridden straight through it on a horse named "Fat Bastard".

She stifled a snort. *Not now, no noise now.* She was tired and needed to get home.

She quietly placed the tray on the small table next to his

chair. Carefully removing the empty cup without making a sound. He was engrossed in something on the television, the subtitles on and the volume muted. Why would she expect any different? His pudgy hand reached towards the tray and found a sandwich. He conveyed it to his gaping jaws, teeth already biting at the air before the food had entered the chewing area.

She felt a slight gagging sensation: there was bile working its way up to her mouth. She had to get out of the room. Get out before she dry heaved, or worse, vomited. Turning swiftly, she clutched the empty cup to her chest and crept out of the room. She quietly pulled the door behind her but was careful not to make the final click of closure.

Upon reaching the safety of her kitchen, she allowed herself a little gasp as she fought to regain control of her errant stomach. She breathed heavily. The water might still be hot enough to help her calm down.

No, she was not doing that again tonight. She could wait until tomorrow for relief. He had been fed and she was out of the room. She checked the kitchen clock. It was almost nine. A couple of minutes to wash the plates then she was done for the night. She could be in her own world until the morning.

Cleaning the few cups in the cooling sink, she quietly stood them on the draining board. The clock's hands had inched past the hour. There was no chime of course, no ticking sound either. Even time ran silently in this house. However, the clock told the truth of the lateness of the hour. It was past nine and she could go. She turned to the back door and picked up her bag ready to leave. Changing into her shoes and putting her slippers to the side, she stepped forward. Cautiously, she turned the handle. She was ready to hear him call out any second now. Those four words which made her brain curl in on itself and brought blood to her face. Any second now.

Nothing.

Silence.

Opening the door, she stepped out into the dark. The sound of her shoes rang across the backyard. Suddenly, she could hear every piece of grit and stone she stood on as she moved from foot to foot. The buzz from a passing mosquito caused her to gasp. Straightening herself and shaking away any trepidation, she gently pulled the door shut behind her.

This time, she allowed it to click shut. She was outside now.

The streetlights made silver pools along the pavement. She passed from one to another, comforted by the sound of her own footsteps. Sounds meant life; she was alive. Silence no longer held her prisoner. Noise no longer betrayed her. For a few short hours, she had free air to breathe. She gulped at the night, tasting the chill that sat upon the air. She raised her nose to the sky and drew in the smells of the street. It felt good to be outside. The sounds of life tumbled and rolled into her periphery. The world came back into focus.

Focus.

Tomorrow, she would continue to perfect her art. She would soon be able to approach his stinking chair quieter than a whispered promise. Soon be able to secure the gluttonous lump so that she was beyond the reach of his piggy little fingers. Those ten little sausages, all wiggly and desperate.

Tonight, though, she had some more reading to do.

She stopped; her hand flew to her mouth.

The book. Had she left it in the kitchen?

Heart banging, she rummaged in her bag, trying to find the book beneath the clutter and used hankies.

It was there! Oh, thank goodness. You silly goose!

Her shopping list was there, too. The one she used as a bookmark. She didn't want to lose this little list, either. It helped her to focus on what she needed.

1. *Cream of Chicken Soup*
2. *Ghee*
3. *Funnel*
4. *Tubing/jug?*

Relieved, she stuffed the dog-eared copy of "*Foie Gras: A Taste for Torture*" back in her bag and picked up her pace. There was still time to catch the late bus if she got a move on.

As she went, her shoes sang a song of freedom into the night.

Satan's Frozen Bum

(Author's note: At the end of "Inferno", Dante and Virgil find Satan trapped up to his waist in the frozen pit of hell. This struck me as being a particularly bad day at the office.)

"Mornin' Boss," said Steve. "Get you a coffee?"

Satan yawned and wished he could scratch his own arse. "THIS BLOODY ICE!" he roared.

Somewhere, below his Satanic Majesty's frozen navel, the botty-scratching officer gave the Foul-One's buttocks a rake over with the designated bum-scritch wotsit.

Satan purred in the manner of a reanimated, soul-sucking feral cat. He closed his amber eyes, stretching his leathery neck and shoulders. His terrible rictus masquerading as a perverse and disturbing smile.

He sighed his grave-dirt tension into the freezing air.

"STEVE!" The Father of Pestilence called out to the demon at the coffee pot, "I'll have a long-black; six hundred and sixty-six sugars. Thanks."

This Small Bird

Once, there was a bird–small, not quite feathered, lost.

This bird was savaged, almost ripped in two.

It fluttered against walls, bins, drainpipes, and into oily puddles, searching for a place of safety. Unable to flee, to escape into the blue, it sought refuge amongst the litter and the discarded. Things of neither value nor use, things it now felt kinship with.

Terrified by the sharp lash of brutal rage that had filled its world, it was unable to long for better times. The fires that would have supplied warmth and light guttered out, dead. Had there ever been a nest or warm wing to shelter under? The small bird remembered only the winter's chill, never any respite.

Eventually, tired and alone, the small bird found a place to sleep. It was a dark place, an abandoned shell.

She, because she was becoming such, buried herself in a corner, inviting sleep to come and hide her from the lash. Others called this place sanctuary too, Odd Birds finding comfort in their bottles and powders. She neither added nor subtracted from their lives, so they tolerated her tiny frame in their darkness.

And so, she stayed, until the darkest part of the deepest night when the monsters came. They had heard of a small bird nesting in the derelict house, and they hungered for her.

"Stay quiet, little one," said a voice in the yawning void that was more than night. "Stay small."

She pushed further into the corner, back against the rotting walls and their meagre protection. The old house shook and creaked in response, and the small bird wished it would collapse upon them all.

But sometimes, even those who believe they have nothing have something, and she discovered so when the Odd Birds stood between the monsters and her little corner. In that dark, a gloom made deeper by the light that should have been, there came the sounds of flesh on flesh, of wood on bone, and the slow squeeze of breath from lungs.

Eventually, the monsters grew bored, frustrated. Thousands of small birds were easier pickings, requiring less effort for greater reward. And so, they took the bottles, the powders and what money those who slept here could beg, and whooped off into the night, back to Leicester Square.

The Odd Birds rose from where they fell and assessed their wounds—nothing serious—before retrieving their hidden supplies.

"They will return for you, little one," said Corky, the tallest Odd Bird.

I wept as the creeping daylight restored my identity and nodded. It was time to go.

Roy, the Budgie Man, put his hand on mine. "We know of somewhere safe for you to go. This is not your world."

On the other side of London, the small bird, me, knocked on a brown door. Recently painted, the number beside shone proudly. Number 8.

The door opened, and a clean-shaven, older man studied me. I wondered why he felt the need to. Was I so foul that people needed to peer through the filth to see the person beneath? A person worth acknowledging?

Suddenly, the door was wrenched further open, and a younger man with soft brown eyes looked at me. A moment later, he was leaping over the threshold to sweep me into his arms.

"Oh, hen," he said in a soft Ayrshire accent, "Come in at once."

That is how I found my sheltering wing. In the home of John and Rabbie, two people with so much love that they had enough left to spare for me.

I was bathed, dressed, and fed, and though I was as unfamiliar to them as could be, they tenderly cared for me, nonetheless. They loved me like they might their own child.

In their care my wounds of mind, as well as body, were given time to heal.

I owe them my life, these people, who welcomed a stranger in, and helped them find their feet.

Eventually, a long time hence, the small bird grew some feathers, left the nest, and made her own way through the perils of life.

No matter the time that has passed, or the miles separating me from then, I will never forget the Odd Birds who protected me, nor the beautiful couple who healed me.

Compassion can be shown to anyone, even the most broken of small birds, and by anyone, even those who have seen so little of it.

In the end, love is love.

A Devil Put Aside

Already?

Time to get up, already? She had only just rolled into bed.

What time was it?

Probably the dog going off, again. Bloody Tyson, that thing is a menace.

Terri's hair lay across her eyes, and her mouth was open, a breath interrupted.

She had been snoring, that was what had dragged her out of sleep. That made sense.

Rolling onto her side, she tried avoiding the judgmental glow of her clock.

Eyes closing again, she sighed.

No. Something else was happening. Someone was here. Somebody was shaking her by the shoulders. One of the kids was awake. Bad dreams again. She pulled the covers to one side, urging them to hop in and snuggle up with her before they properly woke.

When next she stirred, the space beside her remained cold and empty. Lowering her arm, she replaced the covers and opened her eyes to the soupy grey night. A silhouette leant over the bed; a figure framed against the meagre hallway light. There was no time to breathe, let alone scream. Hope died a watery death in her bladder. She wondered if she could get to the kids.

She *would* get to the kids.

"Mum," said the spectre. It stepped back, hands by its side. "Mum, it's me."

She would get to the kids if it killed her. Somehow, she would.

"Mum!" Again the thing spoke, this time leaning in to turn on the bedside lamp. "Mum!"

Illuminated, she recognised the youngster before her, though it wore a waxen mask to hide the hideous rictus that appeared each time the mouth stilled.

Peering into the ashen face, a horrifying realisation crawled into her throat, gloating at the base of her tongue.

"Robbie?" she said, sitting up. "Robbie?"

He nodded. Beneath the frozen features, his eyes were dark as obsidian. "What's happened?"

"Mum, I've killed him." He said it so quietly she almost missed it.

Downstairs, Tyson barked at a car passing by on the quiet street.

The moment stretched.

She took a few more breaths.

The dog stopped yapping.

"Mum, did you hear me? He's dead!"

"I heard you," she replied. "I heard you."

"What am I going to do?" he sobbed. "I'm screwed!"

His dark eyes overflowed, cascades of pain flooding his waxy features, faint colour rising to his cheeks. Somehow it made him more vulnerable, like a rouged porcelain doll. *He's so young, so fragile*, she thought *My little China-doll boy.*

"Sssh!" she said, reaching for him. "It's okay."

She lifted the covers and pulled him in beside her, holding him tightly as he rent himself apart with misery and fear. When he began to calm, she let him tell his story.

Even Tyson kept his silent counsel for the rest of the night.

By the time the sun kissed the morning sky, she had the choreography all mapped out.

The girls ran squealing across the kitchen when Robbie appeared in the morning. Terri may as well have been invisible as they gave him a full rock star welcome.

"It isn't every day you get to have a big brother for breakfast," Terri joked, and told them most kids only had cereal or toast.

Everyone giggled, even Robbie, though she noticed his eyes remained dull. The girls laughed as they flung themselves into his arms, nearly knocking him to the kitchen floor.

"Are you going to take us to school?" asked Etta.

"Pleeeeease?" begged Lilli. "I want to show you the snails."

"Well, I don't know if I can," stuttered Robbie. "Mum, what—?"

"Of course you can," said Terri. "You can make their lunches and walk them both over."

"Yay! I want choc-nut in my sammich, and some cucummer for the snails." Lilli skipped towards the fridge.

"Yuk, Lilli!" said Etta. "Robbie, our class doesn't have stupid snails anymore. I'm in Year 3."

"I'm in Year 1 and we have snails and I love them, and they love cucummer."

"Girls," said Terri. "Let poor Robbie get a coffee and you can tell him all about school. Etta, don't be mean to your little sister. You know how she is about those snails."

Robbie flicked the kettle on, positioning himself at the kitchen table as he waited for it to boil, preparing himself for a year's worth of his sisters' social updates.

As she watched her children from the doorway, Terri knew this innocent chatter would help quieten the other voices singing in her son's mind. Now, it was down to her to do her part and make the music stop. Not looking forward to the day ahead, she headed upstairs to dress.

She hoped she would remember to take everything she needed with her, making two trips would lead to complications.

What if she messed it all up? There was already so much to think about.

Think, Terri. Think.

Oh, God.

By the time she got to the other side of town, workday traffic was just beginning to build. Feeling a familiar biting pain at the back of her lungs, she admonished herself for not taking something for it before she left. It was too late now, the nagging, gnawing agony having settled in for the day. It was as if something was eating away at her spine from behind.

She hated coming here. She hated the feelings that washed over her like dirty water, as though she was lowering herself into a stagnant pool of filthy seepage. After four years, she could still smell the fear on her skin.

But now, he was dead.

Halle-fucking-lujah.

If only it hadn't been Robbie, though. What a mess. Poor kid, just starting out, and that bastard totally stuffed up everything for him by being dead.

Dead.

It kind of suited him, being dead, and she wished she had done the deed years ago. Avoided all those years of being something between a servant and a punching bag. She should have hefted him off a tall building, like a cartoon coyote. *Splat!*

Chuckling softly to herself, she felt a little more in control of the fangs gnawing on her backbone.

Turning into her old street, the small group of people gathered by the corner shop surprised her. She had hoped to slip into the terraced house without being noticed, but there was no chance of that now. She would just have to come back later. Ducking down in her seat, she tried to avoid eye contact with anyone.

"Damn!" she muttered, realising Sally, the only watch-witch the neighbourhood needed, was waving at her. Yes, she was definitely waving.

"Bugger!" she said, waving back. She had no choice, she had to stop. Pulling over, she locked the car and crossed the road.

"Terri!" said Sally, flushed with excitement. "They called you, then?"

Terri couldn't drum up a decent reply, so gave an indeterminate nod, waiting to see what Sally would say next. Her brain was trying to catch up with the new situation. This was not the way it was supposed to go.

Breathe, Terri, breathe.

The spine monkey gnawed harder.

"My Jamal found him, you know," Sally continued, and the gathered group murmured in agreement. They considered this a good thing, Terri surmised, but nobody seemed overly shocked. What was going on?

She gulped.

Gnaw, gnaw, gnaw.

"Saw him through the frosted glass, came and got me."

Nods and murmurs all round.

"Oh," said Terri. That was really all she had at that point.

"Look, long story short, he's had a fall, he's in hospital, and it's not looking great." Sally delivered the news with relish.

"Hospital? What—"

"St Aggy's, about two hours ago. They made a mess of the door getting in, but we'll get it secured."

Terri blinked a few times, surprised there was any of her

backbone left for the monkey to chew on, but it continued frantically gnawing at her spine, the toothy little bastard.

"Door? Broke the door?" mumbled Terri.

Shaking her head to clear the brain fog, she struggled to find any shape in what she had been told.

"Robbie's been away for a few days, hun," continued the nosy neighbour. "We didn't have a number for him."

"Robbie? Right. I'll track him down." Her brain had joined the dance again. "Thanks, Sal, really."

"Listen, we know your old man was a prize arse, but Robbie is a good lad. We didn't want him coming home to that—" trailed off Sally.

She pointed towards the broken front door, which Terri examined properly for the first time. It was just as Robbie had described, even down to the cracked pane just below head height. She gulped and felt the blood drain from her face. The lumbar monkey chewed on with renewed vigour.

"Oh, Terri, you're upset. Still carrying a little candle for him, are we?" Sally sounded almost pleased with the prospect of some added drama.

"No, God, no. It's just a shock, that's all."

Sally nodded. "Of course, dear."

Fumbling with her keys, Terri did the "time to leave" dance. She thanked Sally and her ensemble, gave the door one last glance, and returned to her car.

St Agnes' District Hospital was two miles away. It wouldn't take long to get there. She was unsure what came next, but knew she was in this bloody thing until the music stopped.

The young doctor held the image against the lightbox, pointing at things. It looked like a shadow show, a silhouette of a head with grey and white splodges. She was unsure if she was looking at the thing from above or below. Either way, she did not know what it all meant. It could have been a cauliflower for all she knew. Maybe that was the bastard's problem, he had a cruciferous vegetable for a brain. It would explain a lot. Well, except most cauliflowers weren't violent, vindictive, misogynistic bullies.

She'd tuned out again, what was the doctor saying? Something about bleeding on the brain, that was it. He was bleeding in his brain. He suffered a stroke and sustained a head injury from the subsequent fall down the stairs. It was uncertain if he would survive this trauma. Terri was to prepare herself for a non-favourable outcome. If he survived, the prospect of long-term brain damage was inevitable, the damage to the entire brain significant. In layman's terms, he was buggered. Not quite in a persistent vegetative state, he might notice light and dark, perhaps understand some sounds, but he would no longer participate meaningfully in life.

She appreciated the medic's honesty, noticing the absence of hope in the delivery of his news. Before he left the room, he handed her some information sheets, pressing them into her hand with a wan smile.

What a nice man, she thought.

While she flicked through the leaflets, a nurse appeared, her soft shoes making her arrival silent and surprising.

"Terri?" she said. "I can take you through now, if you're ready."

Terri stuffed the leaflets into her bag and nodded before following the nurse down the corridor and through some double doors marked "No Entry".

Then, she finally saw him, connected to pipes and lines, like a badly designed vacuum cleaner, with bits hanging out, hissing and beeping. She stifled a giggle, turning it into a passable sob, and the nurse laid a gentle hand on her shoulder.

"It's always a bit of a shock, seeing this equipment. I can talk you through it if you like?"

"No, no, I'm fine. Can I just sit here?"

"Of course you can. There's a comfy chair for you. Can I get you a coffee or something?"

"I'd love a cup of tea, if that's okay?"

"No problem, give me a tick," said the nurse, and slipped away as silently as she arrived.

Terri sat at the bedside, staring into the face of her personal monster. Someone had printed his name on the white board above the bed. "Robert T. Slaywood". Next to his name was a smiley face she could not bring herself to look at. She wondered if there was a space to write "Bastard", then gulped down another chuckle. He had never been this much fun to be around when in life.

Stop it, Terri.

The slow hiss and gentle beeps of the machines seemed to soothe her spine monkey, and she felt it slowly clamber up between her shoulder blades, its sharp claws finding purchase in her muscles. Stopping there, it perched just below her jaw, its warm breath in her ear, its teeth chattering in anticipation.

She looked down at the sleeping figure lying supine on the bed. He wasn't long for this world. Digging deep for some pity, she found none.

Oh, well.

A whoosh of air preceded the bone-monkey leaping onto the bed, and she spied it for the first time. It was smaller than she had imagined, its fur a soft brown. However, there wasn't anything cuddly about the thing, not with those talons, teeth and speed. Quickly, it disappeared under the white sheet, and was soon nothing more than a receding lump amongst the tubes.

Beside the bed, a monitor began shrieking. The nurse, returning with the tea, pressed a button to stop the noise.

"Sorry," she said. "I need to grab some meds. I'll be right back."

Alone with him again, Terri smiled. He did not look peaceful anymore. Not surprising really, what with all the other alarms now sounding.

She sipped her tea.

He was slipping away, uncomfortably. It was glorious.

Her little family was finally free of his hideous shade, free and clear of any damage he might do.

Footsteps approached, accompanied by the squeak of trolley wheels.

Terri raised her voice above the increasing cacophony, making sure he would hear her final words.

"Guess what, Robert," she said. "I finally got that monkey off my back."

(Author's note: This short story was inspired by Queen's "Bohemian Rhapsody")

The Wish-Fae

The sharp-edged notebook pressed into Cotty's thigh. The pain flared every time she took a step, making a miserable night even worse.

She had finished all her pre-reading, and completed the online learning, which was how she knew this would be a tedious field trip. Dull for all, unless something exploded or a human managed to capture one of their group. Ahead, Ms Finacle issued last minute instructions, jabbering about code, ethics, culture and other things equally uninspiring.

Eventually, the group arrived outside the Bingo Hall, a "Halloween Bingo Bonanza" banner draped across the entrance, the material fluttering in the October night. The car park was full, and puddles of slick liquid filled the dips in the tarmac. In a nearby doorway, two women huddled, their coats turned up against the wind, and faces lit by their cigarettes' glow.

"Here we are!" said Ms Finacle. "Your base for the evening."

Nine anxious faces stared around while Cotty yawned and adjusted her pointy hat. *Whose stupid idea was it to dress up?*

Finacle continued, "Remember, one wish apiece. Then back to file your field report."

Nine heads nodded beneath their hats. Cotty extricated her hand from under her cloak, giving a thumbs-up.

"Excellent. Now, in you go!"

Ms Finacle cracked the entrance doors a little, and the group quickly slipped inside.

"Cotty," she whispered. "Don't get overconfident. Being visible makes you vulnerable. Many a Wish-Fae has been lost through bad decisions."

"Yes, Miss," answered Cotty as she squeezed through. "I'll remember."

In the foyer, Cotty looked around, disorientated. It wasn't just the sights, the lights, and the frights; it was the sticky carpet, the roar of humans, the thick taste of sweat, and the stink of cheap wine.

Fighting the desire to flee, she stepped into the main hall. As she did, she felt almost assaulted, the volume at such an excruciating level. On stage, a middle-aged man in a shiny jacket had a microphone halfway down his throat. Cotty could not make out what he was saying, only some numbers and an occasional laugh. Judging by the faces of the audience, they were struggling too.

Cotty could not tolerate this torture for long; she would complete her task quickly and leave. Hovering around the tables at the back of the hall, she took in the crowd. Most women were in costume, using Halloween as an excuse to squeeze themselves into sexy nurse outfits or she-devil lingerie.

Ah, that's why we're dressed up! she thought. *We can blend in.*

Despite standing next to people, Cotty remained unable to catch any conversations above the screeching and cawing from the man on the stage.

She spotted a fed-up looking Fairy staring at the man yelling from the bingo caller's podium. Her costume was lack-lustre: wings a-crumpled, her lifeless hair flopped over her shoulders. Cotty approached, safe in the knowledge she would appear as nothing more than an adolescent Trick-or-Treating. The veil thinned on nights like tonight, but was still there, thankfully.

"Hello, missus! I'm your lucky witch, and I'm here to grant you a wish for Halloween," said Cotty.

"What?" yelled the woman above the din.

"I'm here to grant wishes!" shouted Cotty.

"Wish a what? I can't hear you. IS IT A RAFFLE?"

"GRANT YOU A WISH! FOR FREE!"

"A WISH?"

"YES!" Cotty nodded vigorously.

The woman laughed, smiling gently at Cotty. "CUTE!"

Cotty drew her wand from her cloak, checked the charge, and held it aloft. "I'M READY!

"SERIOUSLY?"

Cotty nodded in affirmation, wand quivering.

"OK, THEN. I WISH I HAD LONG, LUSCIOUS LOCKS--"

Cotty began to release the charge, unable to make out the "*beep!*" above the noisy moron on stage.

"—OH YEAH. ALSO SHUT THE ARSEHOLE UP! THANKS!" the woman bellowed as Cotty finally felt the charge shoot through the wand and into the Wish-o-Sphere.

On stage, the shouting stopped, and a cheesy disco tune replaced the man's rant, the volume much lower.

The woman laughed, and she patted Cotty's hat. "You're a clever little witch, aren't you?"

Cotty was silent. She gulped, cold sweat beading her lip.

"Thanks, kid! You made my night. I don't care too much about the hair. The other thing was totally worth it, though!"

"Yep, well, got to go," said Cotty backing towards the door. "Enjoy your evening!"

Then, she was gone.

"You did *what?*" shrieked Ms Finacle.

"I granted two wishes. By mistake, honest. She threw one in just as I was launching," Cotty replied.

"How did they turn out? Did you use the "sleep on it" pause?"

"Yes, Miss. Of course."

"Well, that might be something. Show me your notes." Finacle took the notebook from Cotty's shaking hands.

She read the text silently before handing it back with a sigh.

"The first one is easy enough, but that second one—that one is going to be a real pain in the backside to live with. If you'll pardon the pun."

Cotty stared at the floor.

She shouldn't have been so blasé about everything. That poor woman. Oh dear.

By the end of the evening, Cotty had completed her report and sent off all her paperwork. Both wishes were categorised as body modification, the second falling into the "Significant Impact" cluster.

Judy awoke, the clock showing nearly seven. Time to get up and make Brian's breakfast. She tried lifting her head from the pillow, but it was strangely heavy.

Did she still have that stupid costume on from last night? Fairy Queen. Really?

She sat up and caught sight of herself in the vanity unit. Her reflection showed her face surrounded by silken, chestnut locks that tumbled over her shoulders like melted chocolate on an ice-cream.

Is that my hair?

She ran her hands through the velvet strands, feeling the weight of her magnificent mane. Then she smacked Brian on the back to wake him.

"Look! Look!" she cried.

Brian turned sleepily towards her. Opening his eyes slowly, he made a circle with his mouth and said "Ooh!"

Judy stood, spinning in front of the mirror, admiring herself from every angle.

"What happened?" he asked.

"I made a wish. Well, two, actually. Now I have this amazing hair. Oh my God!"

"You are super-lovely!" said Brian. "I quite fancy you, myself!"

"Ah, give over, silly!" laughed Judy. "I'm going to the loo, and I'll fetch my brush while I'm there."

"Hey, what was your other wish?" he called. He checked his pants in case there had been any improvements overnight. There weren't.

"Oh, I just wanted this arsehole to shut up," she said.

"Oh, right."

Brian swung his legs over the bed and reached for his slippers. He was still perplexed, but nowadays, these beauty products could do pretty much anything if you paid enough. He shuddered as he thought about the cost involved.

A harrowing banshee wail came from the bathroom. He jumped up and ran to the open door to peer in. Seated on the toilet was Judy, screaming and sobbing.

"Are you OK? What's the matter?"

"It's gone," wept Judy. "There's nothing there!"

"What's gone?" said Brian, panic forming in his throat.

"My bum!"

"What?"

"Someone has stolen my arse!"

"Don't be ridiculous. What's going on? First the hair, now this?"

"Someone has sealed my bum up!"

"I'm calling an ambulance, Jude. Stay calm."

Later, a medical intern (who had gone with his mum to the Bingo and wished for an intriguing case) approached a cubicle in the Emergency Department.

He pulled the blue curtain aside.

"Hello, Judy. I'm Dr Reddy. Tell me, what brings you to the hospital today?"

The Jar

If you touch'd your hand to me
would my screams come
blood-wet, through your fingertips
though mute for years?
Would the dusty shadows hiss
filthy, rattled from lungs
collapsing since young hope
gagged on its dream?
Would the sputtered flame of want
spark, try alight
a-fright, contrite? Would it
emerge to bathe in maiden pain?
The answer friend is yes.
Thus, this dome of shame.
The jar enclosing
agonal screaming,
which feasts on me alone.
The saving glass
spares you, kind soul,
from all
but the ghastly view.

Be of good cheer!

We have put it all away again,
into a box marked "Christmas".
The missing ones, the far away friends,
into a box marked "Christmas".

The waiting for mail that doesn't come,
into a box marked "Christmas".
The decorating our empty home,
into a box marked "Christmas".

The wondering how you are getting by,
into a box marked "Christmas".
The little tree that makes us cry,
into a box marked "Christmas".

The candy canes, the silver balls,
into a box marked "Christmas".
The waiting for that never-call,
into a box marked "Christmas".

We'll save our hopes for one more year,
in a box marked "Christmas".
We both are "fine", and of "good cheer",
despite this box marked "Christmas".

We'll carry on, begin again,
and keep our box marked "Christmas".
And we hope next year you'll be here, too,
to open this box marked "Christmas".

Mischief Night

"They had gone, leaving nothing behind them but tyre tracks in the hardening mud, a twist of wire, and the sleepless tapping of the north wind." [1]

Jed peered through the pre-dawn gloom, looking for any signs of the car. He elbowed the man laying spreadeagled next to him.

No response.

Fuck, he thought as he stood and kicked the sleeper's skyward arse again.

"Ugh!" groaned the prone man. "Stop kicking me!" He rolled over and Jed felt relieved to see that, apart from a swollen eye, Mark appeared in one piece.

"I should kick your head in!" shouted Jed. "Look what happened. One of your stupid ideas has gone tits up. As usual."

Mark shrugged, "I thought it went OK, to be honest."

"OK? You're an idiot. We're in the middle of nowhere, and I'm freezing."

Mark patted his robes, frowning, and after checking again, scrutinised the leafy ground. He turned to Jed. "Where's my phone? Can you call it?"

Jed sighed. "We won't pick up any signal out here, but whatever," he said, searching for his own device beneath his fur.

"Bugger!"

"What?"

"I can't find mine either."

"Great, just bloody great!"

"We'll have to walk back."

"Oh, yeah, that's smart, you bloody genius. Look at us!"

Mark had a point. They both wore Halloween costumes. Mark's an obese monk, complete with tonsured hairpiece and brown robes, while Jed sported a gorilla suit without the head. It had been the wrong head anyway, a wolf, not an ape. "No-one will notice, love," the costumier told him as she relieved him of a hundred quid. "Make sure you bring it back in good nick, though."

Now they were in the middle of nowhere, both missing their phones. Hope fading, Jed patted his side. Apparently, he was missing his wallet too.

"Mark, you got any dosh with you? I've lost mine"

His friend fished his card holder out of his front pouch, hidden inside the false belly.

He grinned. "Yup, we're fine."

Nothing is fine about any of this, thought Jed.

It had all sounded so simple when Mark first explained it, although they *were* six pints down at the time.

Halloween was the perfect opportunity to scare the livers out of someone just for fun. The lads planned to carjack a pisshead in a pub car park and drive him around a bit, giving him a fright before dropping him back at the pub. No harm done, and it might make him think twice about drink-driving. It would be a public service, really.

All they needed were costumes, a drunk, and his car. Simple and effective. The lads had chuckled, imagining the drunkard's face when two scary beasties took him for a joyride.

Earlier, sitting in Mark's car behind the Sexton's Castle at closing time, they watched as patrons left; some in taxis, some with designated drivers, and others pulling their collars up against the wind for the walk home. Not everyone wore a costume, but they caught the occasional flash of a cloak or devil tail under warmer outer layers.

Eventually, only one vehicle remained in the parking lot. A dark saloon: its colour hard to define under the streetlights' pitiful glow.

One by one, the pub's downstairs windows darkened.

"Shit!" said Mark. "That must be the landlord's motor."

Jed felt relieved. He was flagging, and the wolf head was itchy and hot.

Mark sat forward, pointing.

"Look!".

A gentleman was being "escorted" out by an employee. He

shoved the man across the threshold and slammed the door behind him.

The man staggered backwards, lurched sideways, and leant against a tree. He looked ready to vomit, and Jed wondered if the costume shop lady would return his deposit if he had puke in his fur.

The drunkard straightened, and peering around, spied the saloon. Walking towards it, slowly but unsteadily, he reached into his jacket pocket, revealing the glint of metal in the low light.

"Keys!" said Mark. "It's his bloody car, alright."

"Oh, God," moaned Jed, "are you sure?"

"Yes, let's go!" With that, the Mad Monk left the vehicle.

Jed the Were-Ape, Dog-Monkey, or whatever, followed reluctantly.

The man was definitely drunk, trying to enter his car via the passenger side. Jed peered through the back window and saw no one at the wheel.

The intoxicated man fumbled with his keys, which jingled and flashed in the gloom. Leaning on the roof, he tried to focus on the door.

Mark jumped forward. One arm raised in a "STOP!" gesture. "Step away from the car!" he cried.

"Wha—?" the man began, "Who the f—"

Mark took the keys from the startled man's hands.

"I am the Mad Monk of Market Hale. I am here to save you." He gestured towards Jed, standing awkwardly to the side. "This is Fang, the Hound of Hell, vicious and vengeful."

"Woof, woof!" barked Jed, feeling stupid. Then he added, "*Grrrr*!" for good measure.

Mark opened the door and pointed to the rear passenger seat. "Get in, if you would, please. We are taking you on a ride to Hell and back!"

The man stumbled and entered the back of the car head-first, feet trailing behind him. There was the sound of scrabbling as he scooted into place. A resounding click echoed.

"Bloody hell," said Jed, "he's even done his own belt!"

Mark winked at him. "So far, so good, I reckon. You drive. Just make sure you can see out of the face-holes."

Jed took the driver's seat, quickly repositioning the seat and wheel before adjusting the mirrors. The pedals sat high, his knees bumping against the steering column. He didn't think the bloke was that small, but maybe he was one of those people that liked pushing their face up to the glass when they drove. *Probably as blind as a bat. Blind and drunk? What a perfect combination.*

Mark jumped into the passenger seat and cried, "Drive on, Hell Hound!"

Jed pulled out and away from the centre of town. There wasn't much in Market Hale—some curry houses, an all-night garage, a medieval church, and the old market square—so he headed instead for the darkened country roads.

The plan was to go a little way out of town, and then drive like a maniac, putting the fear of God into their unwitting passenger. They'd decided that five miles should be far enough.

Mark chuckled at his side, enjoying the escapade, and Jed checked on the drunken stranger in the rear-view mirror. He sat, ramrod straight, his face expressionless, no signs of distress at all.

He's too drunk to know what's happening, thought Jed. *Probably thinks this is a taxi.* Behind the back seats he glimpsed a scurrying movement, something squirrel-like running from one side to the other. He turned back to the road, aware of having swerved in surprise.

"Ha-ha! Stellar work, Hell Hound!" whooped Mark.

"I saw something in the back, on the shelf," he said, voice muffled by the wolf head.

"Don't be a dick. Your dog eyes are seeing things. Keep to the plan. We've got him petrified!" Mark glanced over his shoulder and tried for an evil laugh. The man regarded him coldly, without blinking.

"Fuck, he's *weird*!" said Mark.

Jed nodded, watching the road and the mirror simultaneously. The rigid features of their passenger made his skin crawl.

There it was again! Something skittered off the back shelf and now sat in the man's lap. It was the size of a cat and was growing larger by the second. The man continued sitting, immobile, devoid of expression. Jed veered the car off the road, and slammed on the brakes, causing Mark to lurch forward and groan.

"Calm down! What are you doing?"

Jed could not tear his eyes from the mirror, watching as the impossibly black monkey-thing climbed up on the front headrests. Forgetting that Mark could not see his expression under the mask, he turned to him, face full of terror. On the headrest, the black thing crouched, mouth agape, grinning, perhaps?

Mark stared at Jed in confusion. Then, catching movement out of the corner of his eye, turned to face the thing.

Mark screamed.

Jed screamed.

Mark screamed again.

The thing took up the banshee song and screamed with them both.

It was a monkey, right? No, not an animal at all. More like a pixie or an imp from a fairy story, thought Jed.

Mark held up his plastic crucifix, like a magic charm, and the imp snatched it from his shaking hands, crushing it into powder.

Well, it's not a bloody vampire, thought Jed, and let out a snort of fearful laughter.

The imp rasped and wheezed. It stank of the bottom of rubbish bins, and Mark retched as the smell caught him unawares.

"Do not vomit in my vehicle." This from the stoic backseat passenger. "You," he pointed at Mark. "Step out and get in the back."

Mark glanced across at Jed. His face said that he planned to open the door, as instructed, but run like hell once he did.

Under his mask, Jed's eyes pleaded for him not to leave him alone with the imp and the Corpse Man.

"You will not run, Mark Andrew Deller. You will do as instructed. As will you, Jedediah Merton." Empty eyes flicked from one to the other from the gloom of the back seat.

How can I see his eyes in this darkness? thought Jed. Then he realised this strange man knew their names.

"Fuck!" he whispered under his breath.

The man's tone was flat. "I will repeat myself once more. If you don't comply, I shall incinerate this car, ourselves included. Only Trevor and I shall walk away unscathed."

Trevor growled a satisfied purr, drooling on Mark's shoulder, foul body squirming in atrocious delight.

"Mark, sit in the back next to me. Jedediah, move into the front passenger seat. Trevor will drive. Do it now!"

The lads jumped out of the car. Mark mouthing, "What shall we do?" as they crossed paths in front of the bonnet. Jed shrugged. He was out of ideas.

Back inside, Trevor had readjusted the seat for his own needs. He *tick-ticked* a small growl at Jed while he fiddled with everything. Trevor's face was somewhat feline, but with more teeth than could be counted, and he smelt like shit. Slamming the car into gear, he shot into the road, shedding gravel from the rear wheels.

From the back, Mark whimpered, apparently attempting to apologise but unable to form coherent sentences.

"Shut up, you oaf. You ruined my night, my single night of earthly mischief. I should turn your insides into outsides for the sheer audacity of it."

Trevor took a packet of cigarettes from the glove compartment and placed one between grinning lips. The creature sparked a small flame with the end of a wizened thumb, lit up and inhaled the foul cloud, the smoke adding to the car's miasma. Jed struggled to hold back his stomach again. It was keen on making an appearance.

"You pair of imbeciles totally destroyed my one evening of being almost-human. Once a year. That is all I get." The man leant forward, addressing Jed directly.

"Do you know who I am, Jedediah?"

"No, sir. We picked you at random."

"What about you, Friar Fuckhead? Who am I?"

"Erm— a politician or something?" guessed Mark.

Trevor cackled, pulled on his ciggy, and blew a smoke ring at Jed, increasing his speed.

"Hell's teeth!" the passenger shouted at them, "I'm *His Satanic Majesty!*"

"Isn't that an album by The Rolli—" Mark began.

Trevor screeched a demonic guffaw, taking a sharp, squealing left turn.

Mark fell into His Majesty's royal lap as Jed crashed against the side window.

"Sorry, sorry," Mark said in desperation, straightening up. "I don't know what part of the Royal Family that is, but I did love our late Queen."

"Really? That is your understanding? I'm some minor royal

with a proclivity for shitholes in west Essex?" He slapped the driver's headrest. "Stop here, Trevor. This is far enough."

Trevor stopped as gently as if he had hit a concrete wall. Mark face-planted against the front seat with a thud, Jed's dog head came flying off and dropped into the foot well.

"Everybody out! Now!"

The car emptied instantly.

"Stand over there!" His Majesty yelled, pointing towards some bushes. They complied, fixed to the hedgerow by the car's high beams. The man stood before them, hands on hips, casting a long shadow that slithered towards their feet.

"Let's get this straight," he said. "I am the Prince of Darkness, Lord of the Flies, The Devil, Lucifer..." he stopped as Mark raised his hand.

"Yes?" said the Fount of all Sin.

"You keep yourself busy then," Mark said. "Surely you've got better things to do than bother with us?"

Old Scratch closed his eyes and pinched the bridge of his nose. He sighed, demonically. Trevor lit another smoke and leaned against the car, chuckling and scratching his bony arse.

"I did have better things to do. I planned to buy a kebab, and Trevor enjoys the drive. He likes the girls dressed up as witches, I think."

Trevor beamed a terrifying smirk and made a squelching sound. Jed shuddered.

"But, thanks to you, I am now going home without a kebab and sober. Therefore, you two have to pay."

"Pay?" sputtered Mark. "How?"

"Let's start with your phones, shall we?" Satan held out his hands expectantly.

They handed them over.

"Thank you for these. The best decision you have made so far." He turned to Trevor. "The tools, please, Trevor."

Trevor approached with a hacksaw and chisel, and Mark fell, fainting to the woodland floor.

All Jed could do was scream before all was darkness.

They got back to Market Hale by mid-morning, Jed without his dog head, and Mark having lost the wig and crucifix. The streets were busy.

Approaching the newsagents, they saw a group of people reading papers and examining their phones.

Strange, thought Jed. *Maybe someone famous has died.*

A man noticed them as they approached and shouted, "That's them! The bastards!"

Every head turned their way, staring in anger. Jed and Mark looked at each other, confused. The small group was growing now, echoing with fierce rumblings and cries of "How could you?" and "You should be ashamed!"

The lads put their heads down and tried to power through. One lady, purple hair matching her engorged, furious face, smacked Jed with a newspaper. "Go on," she said, "deny it!"

Jed read the paper shoved into his hands. The front page bore a photo of Mark and himself, naked on top of the church spire. The banner they held read, "'MARKET HALE IS A SHIT HOLE' ~ GOD".

People shoved phones in their faces, showing them clips from the internet. Titles like, "Essex town gets thumbs down from God" and "Almighty Hates Essex - It's Official" abounded. One proclaimed, "Church of England excommunicates Essex without due process".

"Jesus!" said Mark

"Holy Fuck!" said Jed.

"Little shits," said purple lady, "I'll kill you myself!"

"Excuse me! Excuse me!" said a flat, familiar voice, pushing through the crowd. "I shall deal with these miscreants."

Old Nick, wearing a crisp white dog collar, stepped forward. Grabbing them, he guided them to a waiting Daimler, pushing them into the back seats.

The crowd applauded, appeased. "Bless you, Father" came the cry.

The Devil Himself sat in the front seat and nodded to Trevor at the wheel. The imp wore a loose-fitting chauffeur's hat.

"Home please, Trevor. We need to get these two settled in. They are no longer welcome in their old world."

He turned to face them and spoke the last words they would hear as mortals.

"By the way, you are now both called Steve. Get used to it."

[1]Excerpt from "The Looking Glass War" by John le Carré ©D.J.M. Cornwell 1965

Portent Potential

Justin pressed the bell for the third time, the harsh buzzing emanating from behind the frosted glass. Still nothing. No footsteps or voices at all.

Squatting to gain a better view, he lifted the brass letter-box and peered inside. The hallway appeared unremarkable; a jumble of coats on the bannister and a small pile of discarded shoes denoting the bottom of the stairs. Everything was silent; shadows lying still against the walls.

No signs of life.

Nobody home.

He straightened and reached for the bell again, the metal flap snapping back into place with a loud *clang!*

Suddenly, Justin found himself prodding at thin air, the door wrenched open before he could reach the buzzer. In its place, a cardigan-wearing bundle of wrath stood.

Justin gulped. Even though she was not very tall, this lady seemed a formidable opponent. Not only that, but she also appeared extremely cross. Worse still, she seemed cross *at him.*

"You've woken 'em all up!" she hissed. "Idiot!"

"Sorry?" said Justin, unsure of what to say.

"So you should be! Comin' round here, battering on people's doors." She glowered at him, lips drawn back in a half-snarl.

"I'm looking for Brenda Harris," he quickly interjected, holding up his hands as he tried to regain control of the situation. "It's kind of urgent."

"What *kind* of urgent? Proper urgent? Sounds like nonsense." Her death stare did not waver.

"Yes, it is. I mean, not nonsense. Well, it *may* be, but it *is* urgent. Definitely. Yes."
Justin was babbling, sweat drawing lazy lines down his back. *Oh God.*

"I'm Brenda," she said, suspicion in her voice. "What of it?"

Justin exhaled. "Thank goodness. Miss Harris, I've been trying to reach you for days."

"I've been busy, 'aven't I?" she glanced over her shoulder, frowning. "Things to do."

"Miss Harris, sorry to ask, but have you been receiving unusual deliveries recently?"

She snapped around to face him. "What do you know of it?"

Justin took a calming breath and continued, "I'm Justin Bran from Augury Direct. You have been on our recall list for the past two weeks."

"Why? It's not car insurance, is it? I don't even drive."

Justin cleared his throat. "No, it's the—erm—birds, Miss Harris."

"Right, you'd better call me Brenda and get in 'ere, sharp-ish!" She leant out the doorway and checked the street. Then, grabbing him by the sleeve, she dragged him inside and slammed the door shut behind them.

"Sorry, I just has to be a bit careful at the moment, mate. Strange things are 'appening round 'ere."

As she ushered him towards a door at the end of the hall-way, Justin examined his surroundings, noting said door was in need of a coat of paint and a new handle. That seemed the case with everything in the house, though. It was all on the miserable side of well-loved, as if a great romance was over and the divorce was already finalised. All that remained were sad memories of happier times.

In the space beyond, the morning light dripped honey on everything it touched. Dust motes seemingly danced to their own silent tune, rising and falling, riding the air currents like Californian surfers. In stark contrast with the dimly lit hallway, this room, sparsely furnished with only a couple of armchairs and a coffee table as it was, seemed far cosier.

Brenda settled into one of the armchairs, and gestured for Justin to take the other. Squeezing himself in, he adjusted the cushions to achieve some level of comfort. Brenda sighed and folded her hands into her lap, her fiery temper replaced with something far more melancholy. Closing her eyes, her shoulders slumped into the back of her seat.

"Tell me," she said, eyes shut tight. "Tell me what's gone wrong."

"I will in just a second." Justin pulled his phone from his pocket and poked at it. Brenda opened one eye to squint at him.

"Oi! Hope you're not on that bloody Faceblog thing. Thought you was 'ere about them birds."

"No, no, Brenda. Just looking up the inventory list. Don't worry."

Brenda *harumphed* and crossed her arms. When she mumbled something Justin didn't catch, he looked up.

"Sorry? I didn't really hear what you said—"

"I said, it's only a few birds and a cat or two. I'm looking after 'em properly, honest."

"Brenda, according to our records, there are ravens, cats, magpies, frogs, and an owl called Kevin."

Brenda grimaced.

Justin continued. "That's a lot of livestock, Brenda. We've never had to fulfil such a large consignment."

"I got a bit carried away," she replied. "Honest mistake."

"Brenda, do you know why those animals all turned up here?"

"I didn't at first, thought they was just strays. I cottoned on eventually. Bloody bad omens, aren't they?"

"Yes, omens. Sent to warn you about future catastrophes."

Brenda sat forward, her expression animated once more.

"Well, I'm not sending 'em back!"

"It's okay, they belong to you now," Justin replied. "All omens are non-returnable, non-reversible, and non-exchangeable."

"Well, that's alright then," she said, relaxing once more. "That's quite alright."

Justin peered at his phone again, frowning at the tiny screen.

"What is it?" asked Brenda.

"Are you still using MatchMeNow.com?" he asked. "Username of *FriendlyBren*?"

Brenda lowered her eyes, a crimson glow rising from below her jaw to colour her cheeks.

"Not anymore," she said quietly. "Bit of a disaster, really. But I *was* when the birds and things started arriving, though."

"That makes sense," said Justin. "Looks like you had some lucky escapes, judging by some of the people on the site."

"First time, I was off to a date, and I found this raven trapped in the bathroom. Squawking and pooping he was, all over me clean frock. Couldn't go then, could I?"

"Well, that was a clear sign, wasn't it?"

"I'll say! I called to apologise and the fella, Bill, was as rude as you like. Called me all sorts, he did. Bloody good miss, if you ask me. Nasty man."

Justin nodded. "Nothing like a raven in the bathroom to make you think twice."

"After that," said Brenda, "every time I planned a date, some creature or other would pop up and get in the way. Cats, frogs, birds; it was never ending."

She shook her head, chuckling to herself.

"All I wanted was a nice gentleman friend for some company. Getting a bit lonely as I gets older, you see. Then, before I knows it, I'm having me own zoo and no time for people."

"But you kept making dates on the site. Why would you do that if you already had plenty of animals to look after?"

Brenda gave Justin a quizzical look, studying him closely. He felt her appraising him, and wondered how he appeared in her eyes. He had the benefits of longevity that working in the Quasi-Natural sector came with, which knocked a decade or so off his appearance. Even so, he estimated Brenda was at least thirty years his senior.

"Justin," she said, after a long pause. "I worked out that each time I chose the worst of the worst from MatchMe— the real 'orrible, vicious buggers—I'd get another creature, as a warning. Understand?"

Justin shook his head. "Not really."

She laughed, getting to her feet.

"Come with me," she said, and pointed to the door.

Across the hallway, Brenda ducked into a recess beneath the stairs, gesturing for Justin to follow. He had to crouch a little, only to find himself in front of an imposing security door, which Brenda quickly unlocked.

"Have a look," she said, stepping back.

Justin leant in, surprised that the space was far bigger on the inside than it rationally should be. He made note of the occupants, the cages, the feeding apparatus, and the ventilation system. It was a good setup, well thought out, and appropriately sound-proofed.

He nodded his approval and stepped back out, moving to stand next to Brenda in the hallway.

"Well?" she said.

"It's brilliant!" said Justin. "What a great solution."

"All I had to do was find the complete bastards, arrange a date, and then *wham!* I got a nice new raven or kitty-cat for company. Easy-peasy really!"

Justin couldn't contain his grin. *Well done, Brenda,* he thought.

"Righto, let's show you where I keeps me pets," said Brenda.

She led Justin through to the conservatory, where they were greeted by a mob of furry and feathered creatures.

"Here they all are," she said. "Well, all 'cept for Kevin. He's in the loft 'til dusk. Silly old owl."

A black cat wound itself between Justin's ankles, creating a figure eight while purring loudly, its tail flicking like a conductor's baton.

"I'll put the kettle on," said Brenda. "Make yourself at home, but watch out for bird poop on the seats."

Hurrying off towards the kitchen, she was keen to play host for the first decent company she'd had for a while. He was such a *nice* young man, so polite. She hoped the magpies would behave themselves whilst she was out of the room, no nicking stuff and that. She wondered if there were any fancy biscuits left in the tin. This was going to be a lovely day; she could just tell.

As she passed the bottom of the stairs, she glanced towards the security door.

Bloody vicious bastards.

Worst of the worst?

"Not anymore, you're not," she giggled. "Didn't see *that* coming, did ya?"

Teaser

Here is a short scene from my current work in progress.

No context is provided.

Enjoy.

The Interview

The youth lounged against a strut; uninterested in the conversation taking place in front of him. If there was an Olympic event for being insipid, he would have won the gold.

He shifted from one foot to another. His clumsy black boots were scuffed and worn across the studded heel. His skinny jeans strategically ripped, enhanced with metal accoutrements. He wore an old black hooded jacket with faux-Norse iconography across the back.

Under the hood, his skin glowed anaemically in contrast to his kohl-blackened eyes. Pale hands were stuffed into pockets. He had all the charms of yesterday's porridge. He watched on insipidly as the other two continued their argument.

Paul threw his hands up in exasperation. He sucked air through his teeth and blew it out sharply. "Well, you have to take him!" he hissed.

"No, I don't," Linda said, calmly sipping at the last of her coffee.

"*You* bloody well asked for an assistant. Not *me!*"

"I've already got one," she replied. "You arranged it yourself."

"This—" Paul gestured wildly at the sullen youth who was picking at his spots. "This is what I have arranged."

Linda turned to survey the newcomer. She clicked her fingers and waved him over. He lolloped halfway across the room, then stopped as if his battery had died.

Linda sighed. "Stand there."

She pointed at a spot in front of her desk. The boy stood slack mouthed and looked at Paul.

"There!" Linda repeated, pointing. "Are you a cretin?"

"Er no, I'm a Taurus." the boy said as he drew closer.

Linda rolled her eyes. "You're a Goth, aren't you?"

"Well, no, not really. I'm a bit more Industrial Techno than pure Goth. Unless it's a requirement then, *yes*, I'm a Goth." The boy grinned, revealing the teeth of an octogenarian.

Linda sucked in a deep breath then turned her furious gaze towards Paul.

"Get. Him. Out." she said flatly.

"Really?" said Paul.

"Yes, really. Do it. Now!" Her teeth clenched together, hibiscus pink leeching into her palé skin.

Paul turned to the boy, who was grinning inanely. "You'll have to go now, Rozzer."

"Rizla, my name's Rizla," he replied. "You promised me a dip into the Dark Side. Cavorting and a bit of casual sinning, you said."

"I know I did, Roswell, but I've changed my mind. No more to be said!"

"Rizla, not Roswell."

"Whatever— The deal's off, Ratso. Now, off you pop."

"It's Rizla, and I want to cavort. You promised!"

His bottom lip hung over his chin at the injustice of the thing.

"No. Final warning. Bog off, Rizzo."

"It's Rizl—"

"BOY!" boomed Linda in a voice from the core of the earth. "BEGONE!"

Rizla was gone.

"Thank goodness," said Paul.

"That was *your* mess, not mine." said Linda. "Now, bring me another coffee then piss off."

ABOUT THE AUTHOR

Rachel's passion for words began when her father crafted her a bed out of a bookcase.

This magical place was where she first dreamt of writing her own stories.

Creativity, imagination, and wit run through the family genes.

She is thrilled to include a poem from her nephew, Isaac, in this anthology.

Her preferred genre is comedic horror. She has yet to find anyone that wants to read it.

With that in mind, she dabbles in other things - darting about like a spaniel at breakfast buffet.

She lives with her long-suffering husband, Steve, in Katherine, Northern Territory, Australia.

He hopes she makes a fortune selling her books because he would like to retire early.

CONTACT

Blog: rachelkjones.me

Facebook: www.facebook.com/jonesyagain

Bluebird of misery: twitter.com/JonesyWriteNow

Amazon author profile: www.amazon.com/author/rkjones

www.ingramcontent.com/pod-product-compliance
Lightning Source LLC
Chambersburg PA
CBHW020529120726
47904CB00003B/1017